APOCALYPSE THE BELIEVER

THE POWER OF TWELVE BOOK THREE

MIRANDA MARTIN

CONTENTS

FOREWORD

Don't miss the start of *The Power of Twelve* start at the beginning if you missed it!

Apocalypse: The Beginning
By Miranda Martin

CHAPTER ONE

AVIELLA

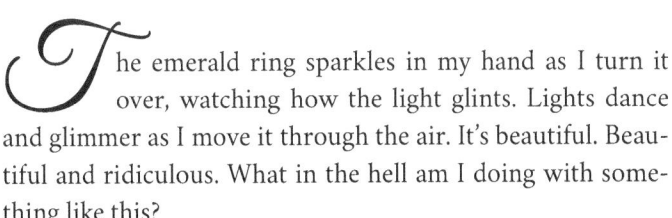

*T*he emerald ring sparkles in my hand as I turn it over, watching how the light glints. Lights dance and glimmer as I move it through the air. It's beautiful. Beautiful and ridiculous. What in the hell am I doing with something like this?

Me. An orphan. Left behind by my dad, just an ordinary girl. At least, I thought I was, but that was before. So much has happened since I could lay claim to being 'just a girl' that it seems like it was a lifetime ago.

My entire room is untamed opulence. Ridiculous, over the top, more than I need and more than I want. It makes me uncomfortable having so much spread around me, knowing damn well that there are masses a level below that are barely surviving.

Welcome to the Apocalypse. Everything went to hell, literally, and those of us who are left are trying to survive. Okay, that's not true, everyone else is trying to survive. I'm trying to figure out my fate.

Who am I? Why am I special?

There's no point in trying to deny it anymore. Self-delusion isn't cute and has zero value. It's another one of those things, face it or act like an idiot and deny the truth. The freaking Horsemen of the Apocalypse have told me I'm special, that the fate of the world is in my hands.

There it is again.

Their words echo in my head when I think of them. The familiar buzz, *It* as I used to call the sensation when I was a kid, but now know it's my magic, thrums through my limbs and in my blood. The hair on my neck and arms stands on end. Okay, it's weird, I don't know what to do with it or about it.

The fate of the world.

Shuddering, I close my hand over the emerald ring, balling it into a fist. I raise my arm back to throw the silly thing against the wall but I stop myself. What's the point? I'll have to pick it up. If I don't, Sam, the girl who sneaks in here to clean my room will.

I know she sneaks in because even though I never see her, the room is cleaned anytime I'm out of it—bed made, clothes straightened, and worse, there are new things added almost every time. Gifts from Tynan, Dragon Horseman of the Apocalypse and ruler of this bunker.

I'll catch her sooner or later. She's good, but once I set my mind to something, I get it.

I rise to my feet and drop the ring on the dresser as I pass it by. It lands among the refuse of the other pieces of jewelry the Dragon has bestowed upon me. Sighing, I shake my head, frustration swamping my thoughts.

Turning in a slow circle, I let my eyes drift across all of this… stuff. Anger pulses inside like a throbbing bass drum. This is a waste of time. I should be out there finding my dad. They want me to save the world, fine, but first, I need Daddy. This game of waiting is coming to an end. I'm not going to put up with it any longer.

What good is saving the world if I can't save him?

Sighing, I throw myself onto the overstuffed bed, sinking into the luxurious mattress and jerk the down-filled comforter over myself. Closing my eyes, I try to relax. Listening to my heart and breathing helps, a little. I know I can't go, not yet, I don't know nearly enough.

My thoughts, which I can't keep from my dad, drift back to the beginning. Before all of this there was the two of us. I didn't know that my life was strange, not back then. What did I have to compare it to? Didn't all little girls live on the road with their Daddy?

We never stayed in one place for long. A couple of months at the most before we'd be on our way again. He taught me a lot. Somehow, he knew what was coming. I remember asking him once how he knew so much. He smiled, that loving smile that made his eyes light up, and shook his head.

'Your Mommy told me,' he had said.

'Where is she?' I'd asked.

'In Heaven, watching over you, because you're so special.'

The next part I can't recall, but there's something about that moment. Squinting my eyes tightly, I try to recall what it was he'd said next. Strange that I can't. It won't come at all though. Something about me and my mom.

"Gah!" I exclaim, leaping off the bed and landing on my feet.

Magic buzzes in my gut. Action. I need to do *something,* anything!

I pace my rooms from one to another—I've an entire suite of them. Which also bothers me. I grew up in an orphanage with four girls to a room. Humanity lives underground hiding from the unleashed monsters and the war between the angels and demons above. Space is at a premium and here I am with enough space for at least twenty.

Tynan. Jerk.

Sexy, super-hot, undeniably delectable, and oh-my-god do I want to…

No, shut that thought down right now. No way, no how. I am *not* going to get involved with him any more than I am. No matter how nice it would be… and a girl has…

Nope. Nope. Nope.

Shaking my head, I walk towards the shower. Maybe cold water will cool my jets. I've got too many men and not enough of me to go around. Adding in the Dragons, which I almost can't admit even to myself almost happened, is too much. Isn't it?

Shut it Aviella. Shut the living hell up.

Where is Rowan when I need her? Hanging with the mages, who are also so fricking hot…

So, about that saving the world gig? There, that kills the horny buzz.

Me. Little Aviella, savior of the world. Right.

Delusions of grandeur, yeah? Except it's not my delusions. It's theirs—Efram, Silas, Tynan, Killian, Rafe, and all the rest. Closing my eyes, I feel them. The connection I have with each of them is as real as the cold handle of the shower faucet in my hand. Alive, electric, and filled with possibility.

Crazy or not, I'm connected to them and they all believe I'm something. Something special, something to believe in. I strip out of my clothes, let them drop to the floor, and step into the shower.

"Woah," I gasp, as the cold water hits me.

When I lean my head back, the spray runs over my face and down my hair, which is growing longer. I haven't had time to cut it or do anything with it in a while. I should find a band or something to bind it back with. If I do get in a fight, I don't want it getting in the way.

If I get in a fight. Huh, like there's any doubt I will. The sooner, the better actually. At least then I'll be doing something!

Another Seal has broken. An army of monsters is stampeding across the earth, and here I am, hiding away with the Horsemen of the Apocalypse and some of my friends. Neatly tucked away and protected on all sides. If I'm supposed to be the big savior, why won't they let me out there to stand against the nightmares that plague the survivors?

Because I'm not ready, of course.

"You know," I say to myself. "Talking to yourself is crazy." When I shake my head, droplets of water fling in all directions.

"Nope," I answer. "Not answering yourself, that's crazy. How rude do you have to be to not answer yourself?"

Snorting at my own joke I turn around and let the water beat down on my shoulders. There's a knock on the door. I jump and slip, barely keeping myself upright.

"Damn it," I mutter, stepping out of the shower. Wrapping a towel around myself, I go to the door, wet and irritable.

"Wha—" I cut off mid-word.

Efram's eyes widen, his lush lips part, and his tongue stops between them. His eyes drift down my exposed flesh. Goosepimples rise all over my skin as a chill races down my spine. My core tightens, my breath catches, and I can't help noticing the rising bulge in his pants.

Neither of us says a word, staring one at another, waiting for… something. My magic stretches. It's an awareness I'm still learning to comprehend, strange sensations and understandings. It brushes with his, intertwining, an energy that crackles between us. Warmth flushes my cheeks and chest, and a new shiver hits me from the cooling air. It jerks me into motion at last.

"Hi," I say, breaking eye contact first and stepping to one side to let him in. "Let me… dress."

I hesitate on the word, wanting, oh so badly, to say something completely different. Resisting my urges is getting harder and harder. The connection between Efram and me is strong, maybe stronger than with the others. How do I tell? Worse, how do I choose?

"Yeah, good idea," he says, his voice husky.

Holding the towel in place, I walk into my bedroom and do my best not to sway my hips any more than I must. I fight the urge to drop the towel and throw myself into his arms.

Lucky girl, all these hunky guys wanting you. Except it's not so lucky is it? If it was a matter of sex only, it'd be lucky, maybe. It's not, it's so much more. My feelings for each of them are deep, so deep I can't stand the idea of hurting any of them, and if I choose one, I will. There's no way around it.

Besides, how do I choose only one? Each of them has something different and unique that pulls me to them. We're all connected, intertwined, brought together by whatever fate lies in store for me.

There's a mood killer, I think, throwing the towel to one side and opening my closet. The wardrobe is packed with clothes. I swear Tynan sends more every day, as if that's going to placate me. I snort. He doesn't know me at all.

After digging through them for a while, I find a pair of jeans and a sweatshirt at last, deeply buried among all the over-the-top finery. Once they're on, I walk back out to Efram, feeling composed enough to keep myself under control.

"Hi," I say again as I enter.

His jaw tightens, his eyes roam over my body before locking on mine and keeping them there. I can see the tension in his shoulders, the stiffness in his back. The bulge in his pants is gone and I sense the change in him, in his energy. He's holding back, hard.

Okay, if that's the way it is.

6

It doesn't matter in the slightest that I know damn well it's for the best, it annoys me.

"Hi," he says, his voice sounding absolutely normal now, all hints of the earlier tension gone. "Thought I'd check in on you, see how you're holding up?"

Shaking my head, I shrug. "It's all here," I say, motioning around with a hand. "Every luxury I ever dreamed of in the orphanage. Empty and meaningless."

"Oh?" his eyebrow arches and his head tilts to the side.

"Yeah," I shake my head. "I want out of here. Now. My dad is out there. I need to go, get out there, and find him."

"I get that," he says.

The words carry so much more than they would from anybody else. His understanding is real, it echoes inside, comforting me with a spreading warmth, like a soft blanket I want to snuggle up in.

Silence settles as we sit, and I can't think of anything more to say. Bouncing my leg, I look for some topic to steer the conversation in a different direction.

Something besides the urge I'm struggling with to kiss him. The wondering what his lips would feel like on my skin. The sensation of his touch exploring....

"How about we take a walk?" Efram asks, thankfully interrupting my train of thought.

"Yes!" I say, too enthusiastic, but so grateful for anything to end the awkwardness.

He smiles, as if he knows what I'm thinking, and rises to his feet holding his hand out. It's a chaste gesture, no matter how much more my burning itch might want to read into it. I take it, and we walk out into the society of the Bunker.

This particular bunker is different than the others I've been to, on the surface at least. I've been here long enough to see past the gilded facade to what lies underneath.

Only on closely looking do you notice that all the pretty

dolls are too skinny. Or see the marks on their arms where they've cut themselves in acts of self-mutilation and revulsion. No, it's no better here than anywhere else, no matter how much pretty paint they lay over it all.

Tynan's work, I know. He doesn't want to see the true horrors of the Bunker he is the de facto ruler over. Of course that leads to a further thought...

"I've spoken with the Coven some more," he says.

The Coven. A group of witches operating in the Bunker underground. Every Bunker I've been to has had some form of resistance happening. Maybe that's part of human nature too.

"Yeah?" I prod him along.

"Yes," he says. "They don't trust the Dragons."

"Big surprise," I observe.

He glances at me with an unreadable look. My best response is to ignore it.

"You trust them?" he asks, after we've walked quite a ways in silence.

Frowning I think about that. Do I? No, yes, maybe, sort of? None of those are an actual answer.

"I don't think they want to be horsemen," I say instead of directly answering.

"What?" Efram asks, stopping and turning his full attention to me.

Shaking my head I stare out at the crowds of people wandering the halls of the bunker. They put themselves on display, hoping to be noticed by someone of higher rank than they are.

The area we've stopped in is an open space with four tiers rising up. Walkways circle the area as it rises up to a lit and painted ceiling that gives the illusion of sky, if you don't look too closely. You don't have to look very long to see the effect is a trick of painting and lights moving across it to simulate clouds moving across the open sky.

Hundreds of men and women prance around like ponies on display. Proudly putting themselves out there as if their gaudy clothing, makeup, and carefully coiffed hair is all that matters. Each of them the center of the universe, in their own minds at least.

Do none of them see what they are doing? My anger roils, a welcome distraction from the harder questions that Efram is forcing me to look at. If any of them would give a single damn about anything more than themselves, then this place would almost immediately become better.

"Aviella," Efram says, his voice cutting through my distraction. "What do you mean? Do you trust them?" The disbelief in his voice is obvious.

"Sort of," I shrug. "There's something more to them, something I haven't figured out yet."

"What happened between you and them?" he asks, his eyes flashing steel and his jaw tightening.

I drop my eyes. I can't meet his gaze. This is one of those things I don't want to tell him. My skin itches and desperately I look for anything to get out of the conversation.

"Nothing," I dodge. "Nothing, really..."

His magic crawls along my skin, and I know he knows I'm lying. Well, I'm not lying, I didn't sleep with them or anything. Barely.

"Aviella," he says, his voice low and hoarse. "You have to trust me. Please."

The note of pleading in his voice cuts through all my worries and concerns. Efram is my oldest friend. The only one I have that I know, one hundred percent, I can trust, now that Rowan has gone with the mages for training and protection.

"Yeah," I sigh shaking my head.

I spot a food stand, so I walk towards it, letting Efram fall in beside me as I step up and order a drink.

When the seller looks up to say the price, his mouth drops open and his eyes widen. "Of course!" he sputters, grabbing the coconut flavored water and handing it to me.

I hold out the credits to pay for it, but the man shakes his head, holding up a hand.

"No, no," he says. "For you it's on me."

Rolling my eyes I turn away, muttering about Tynan and his overbearing need to control every aspect of my life. The look on Efram's face matches what I'm sure is on my own.

"You were saying?" he prompts.

Sipping the drink, I walk away and into the crowds with him at my side.

"When the seal broke I was with them, there was a moment, then, that I shared a telepathic connection with the three dragons."

"A connection? Telepathic?" Efram parrots my words back at me.

"Yes…"

"Are you sure they're not putting those thoughts into your head?"

Frowning, I think about that as we stroll along the promenade. Could it be? Sure, of course it could. They're freaking dragons for all that's holy, oh and let's not forget, they're the Horsemen of the Apocalypse. God's Will given horrible form, or some such thing.

No matter all that, though I don't think that's the case. No, I'm certain it's not. I don't think they could.

I don't know why I believe this, but I do.

"No," I say, shaking my head, speaking out loud after I give the entire thing some serious thought. "I don't. I don't understand what they do want, yet, but they're not happy with their current role."

"Okay," Efram says, neither believing me or choosing to not argue further. "Be careful, Aviella. They're dangerous, no matter if they are or not."

As if on cue to his words there's a disturbance. A buzz runs through the crowd, and my magic senses hum. It only takes a moment for me to spot the source. Alaric and Shen, another two of the Dragon Horsemen, walk along the second story promenade. They're surrounded by their 'darlings' and a gaggle of aspiring 'darlings'. Beautiful young girls and women who have starved themselves half to death, to the point it's almost grotesque, in my opinion. It's all part of their desire to be close to power, no matter how tangentially.

There's no denying the power that exudes from the Dragons. They walk along, deep in conversation with each other and ignoring everyone around them.

"Don't stare," Silas says from over my shoulder, causing me to jump.

"Wha—"

He cuts me off with a look. "Bunker Two has fallen," he says, his voice barely above a whisper. "Alaric and Shen set their surviving population free, taking only their 'best' with them when they came here."

Despite Silas' warning, I stare up at the two Dragons. What are they up to now?

CHAPTER TWO

EFRAM

*W*e follow Silas through the crowds to the small office that Tynan has given him. Once we're inside he locks the door behind us then leads the way through another locked door.

This is obviously his inner sanctum. All four walls are covered with floor-to-ceiling shelves loaded with books and skulls.

As soon as I enter the spirits of the skulls whisper to run. It's a ploy, one I know well.

They're trying to make the newcomers feel fear which they then feed off of in an attempt to grow stronger. The spirits making portals out of the skulls are bored and only putting a half-hearted effort into it. It's obvious they've been trapped here for a long time and not well fed.

I walk over and touch one of the skulls lightly, opening a more direct line to the attached spirit.

Who?

'Let it go,' I command it. 'Be free.'

Free?

'Yes, go free,' I order.

It resists, fear gripping it, a common problem with spirits, especially ones that have been stuck for a long time.

'No fear,' I say. 'Go free.'

It quavers in my head resisting the command so I channel my magic into it pushing the spirit away from its connection. The connection is already tenuous from age and not having fed, it doesn't take much for me to drive it out.

"How do you know Bunker Two fell?" Aviella asks.

Silas stops beside his desk and looks sad.

"I have resources," he says simply.

"But... all the people..." Aviella's pain is obvious, on her face and in her voice.

Moving next to her, my urge to protect her swelling but there's nothing I can do for her against this pain. She cares, too deeply sometimes. Somehow she feels responsible for every bad thing that happens in the world.

"He gave them two trains," Silas says, sliding down into a seat behind the desk and motioning that we should do the same.

"Two trains?" Aviella asks. "That wouldn't hold, what, twenty percent of the population?"

"Perhaps, a bit less or a bit more," Silas agrees.

"All those people..." she trails off.

"That's not why I brought you here," he says pointedly.

"What happened to it?" Aviella asks, not being diverted so easily.

"Trumpet creatures," Silas answers. "They're going after all the bunkers."

"We have to stop them!" Aviella says, leaping to her feet.

Her magic rises, filling the room, causing the hair on my arms to stand on end. It's static electricity, intertwining with my own magic, drawing me in. She does it without even realizing what she's doing.

Looking at Silas, I see she's doing the same to him. Her

eyes flash dangerously, moving between the two of us. It's sensual and erotic, her magic the touch of a lover caressing my skin as it passes over me.

Drawn to her, I rise, involuntarily moving closer. Silas moves around his desk, pulled in by the gravity that is her.

"Aviella," he says, his voice tight as he struggles against her.

"Stop," I say, so close to her we're almost touching.

Silas is on the opposite side of her and I want nothing more than to touch her, kiss her, to feel her skin on mine....

"No!" she exclaims. "We've sat here too long. We have to go out there, find my Dad, and stop this. We have to stop it before anyone else gets hurt!"

She still doesn't see the effect she's having on Silas and me. The love she has for people she's never met, the concern for others, everything that she is. She's so... perfect.

"Get. Control. Now," Silas says, struggling with each word as his hands lightly touch her arm then slide down it sensuously,

Jealousy stabs into my heart, and involuntarily, I growl, reaching out and touching her opposite side. Unwilling to let him have that contact unless I, too, get to touch her.

Aviella stops as Silas and I touch her. She looks at his hands then at mine, her mouth dropping open. Her magic embraces both of us, a light touch, caressing, pulling out desire and love.

Biting her lip she takes a step backwards, closing her eyes, and shaking her head.

"I'm sorry," she says, as she struggles for control too.

"It's fine," Silas says, straightening his shirt and walking back around the desk as if nothing happened.

I mimic him, though I feel anything but the level of control he displays. I hope it doesn't show that I'm nowhere near as in control as I want her to believe. The effect she has on me is overwhelming.

She sits back in the chair, apparently oblivious to her own power. It's not just her magical power, though that's considerable, it's her. Her heart, her love, her beauty that affects us all.

"Do you know how many survivors there were?" she asks, staring at the floor.

"No," he answers. "I'm sorry, I don't have that information."

She purses her lips, hangs her head, she mutters, "Damn it."

Silas and I exchange a look and wait for her to process. If nothing else, her strength is always surprising. She sighs, straightens, and looks at both of us in turn.

"Sorry," she says.

"It's fine," Silas says, waving it away with a hand gesture. "I knew you'd want to know."

"Right," she agrees. "Well, what else? Any word from Nathaniel and Rafe?"

"Nothing yet," he says, picking up a book that rests on the desk. "I did find this for you."

He hands the book across, and I look with interest as she takes it from him.

"It tingles," she comments as her fingers close around it.

Silas nods as if he expected that. She opens it and flips through the pages. I can't read the script in it but I do recognize the symbols that she drew from her vision. She stops on a page and traces the symbol with her fingers.

"I can't read it," she says.

"I expected that," Silas says, his fingers tapping lightly on the desk. "When you can read it, it should prove useful."

"When I can?" she asks.

"Yes," Silas agrees. "I believe that your awareness is expanding. Over time you will come to understand these symbols, and when you do, I suspect this writing will be clear to you as well."

"Well that's a tall order," she quips.

"I'm sure you can fill it," Silas says, serious as always.

"Great," she sighs, shaking her head. "Anything else?"

"Unfortunately, no," Silas says. "All of us are working to decipher the symbols and to figure out what is going on. We need you to be patient."

"Patience," she growls. "It's a commodity I'm running short of."

"I understand," Silas says, his eyes darting to me with a momentary look of pleading.

I know what he's asking of me. I'm supposed to keep her distracted so she doesn't do something. When Aviella does 'something' it has, historically, turned out to be very big and game changing. Since we're still trying to figure out what game we're even playing, changing it up or tipping our hand isn't a good idea.

"My dad is out there," she says. "I'm not waiting much longer."

"Believe me, we're working as fast as we can," he says.

Silas is in touch with the Mage Cabal and the Dragon Horsemen, all of whom have pledged themselves to helping Aviella.

More than that, I know the Methuselah is a good man. He's been alive for hundreds of lifetimes, but one thing about him, when he gives his word, he considers it binding.

None of that lessens the ache in my chest when I catch the way he looks at Aviella or when I have to feel his desire pulse through his magical energy.

I can't blame Silas though. We all want her. Someday, probably soon, she's going to have to start choosing. The effect she has on each of us is going to push it to a head, sooner or later.

"Right," she says. "I'm hungry. Anyone joining me for lunch?"

"I'm sorry, I have to get back to work," Silas says.

"I will," I say, accepting my duty and the duress of being in her presence while being unable to tell her how I feel.

"See you, Silas," she says as we leave his office.

We walk back to the main promenades and find a vending machine where we buy food. Aviella looks around at the small tables set up for eating, and she sighs.

"Mind if we go to the room to eat?" she asks. "I can't stand looking at all these starving waifs while I stuff my face."

"Sure," I smile.

We go back to her rooms because they're bigger and nicer than the room I have for myself. Tynan has held nothing back when it comes to her.

We eat the food in relatively comfortable silence. When she finishes the last of it she leans back in the chair and stares at me.

"Do you think they're okay?" she asks.

There's no question in my mind who she's referring to.

"Yes," I say.

"How can you be sure?" she asks, concern written across her face and in her voice.

"Because they've both been at this longer than both of us together have been alive. Nathaniel is an angel and Rafe is a demon, who or what do you think is going to take on either one of them, much less the two of them together?"

"Yeah," she says, biting her lower lip. "Well if nothing else, Rafe will annoy them to death, right?"

"You've got that right," I laugh along with her. "Avi, they're fine. Trust me. They'll be back soon enough."

She gives me a half smile and a nod before stretching and yawning.

"You want to take a nap?" I ask.

"I didn't sleep well," she admits.

"You can go lie down, I'll stand guard if you want," I offer.

She looks up, meeting my eyes, and fidgets nervously.

"Would you... lie with me?" she asks, her voice soft.

It's perfectly clear this isn't an offer for what my body so desperately wants. She's asking for a friend, a protector. She's asking for me.

"Of course," I say without hesitation.

She gives me a grateful smile, and we walk into her bedroom together. She climbs onto the bed first and curls, wrapping herself around a pillow. Once she's settled I get on the bed and wrap myself around her.

The sweet scent of her fills my nostrils as she snuggles against me. She fits like a glove. As if this is where she was always meant to be.

No matter how much I want her, I can't take advantage of her like this. She's being worn down by the mystery of her father, the stress of our situation, the weight of her fate lying on her. No, when I take her, if I ever do, it has to be right. It has to be because she chose me, not for some momentary comfort.

CHAPTER THREE

AVIELLA

J wake up in Efram's arms, his warm embrace comforting me. Carefully I slide out from under his arm and slip off the opposite side of the bed, doing my best to not wake him.

Staring at his sleeping form my emotions are a weird, volatile mix. I appreciate that he didn't try anything, but damn it, I want him to try something.

He's too sweet, and I know it. I'm not going to blame him for being who he is. Him being who he is—it's why I feel this way about him.

When I slip out of the bedroom and into the sitting room, breakfast waits on the table for me, as usual. It's creepy, knowing that someone was in my rooms while I slept. It doesn't matter if I lock the door. I've even blocked it off to no avail.

Lord grant me the strength to accept the things I cannot change, right?

Sighing, I sit down at the table and fix myself a plate of fresh fruits, cheese, and small, biscuit-like things that I'm sure have some fancy name I don't know. All other things set aside, the food here is delicious.

"Sorry I overslept," Efram says, sleepily stretching in the doorway.

"No problem," I say. "Breakfast?"

He nods and sits down, helping himself. The consuming of food lets us avoid small talk. I'm not upset about that, my thoughts are consumed with how I can get about finding my Dad. I didn't dream of him last night, which is a change, but it doesn't move him any further from my thoughts.

"I have things I need to do, will you be okay?" Efram asks as we finish the meal.

"Sure," I say, looking around the luxurious room. "What else could I be?"

He grimaces at my sarcasm but accepts and it we say our goodbyes.

And so another day begins. Another long, boring day of waiting. Waiting and worrying. The weight of the world is literally on my shoulders, and what do I do? Play solitaire. Yep, that's how the fate of the world is being decided. A lone orphan playing solitaire.

I can't focus on the cards. I pass some time pacing the room, and eventually most of the day has passed while I read an old romance novel that I barely pay attention to the words. There was a part of it that was interesting for a moment, as it turns out the book was a 'reverse harem'.

Great—for a book.

Did Tynan send this book to me on purpose? That train of thought went dirty fast, so I pull myself out of it, pushing away memories of my very short time with the three dragons right before the trumpet sounded.

No point in getting all hot and bothered about it again. I can't let that happen. Too much rides on me and my decisions. One thing I know is, I can't do this alone. I'll need all my companions to pull off... whatever it is that I have to do.

Vague. Ugh. Maybe that's the real problem? We don't know who or what we're up against nor do we know what we have to do in order to save the world.

Which of course brings it all back to the fact that I could be nuts. Delusions of grandeur precipitated by the loss of my father, oh! and the minor inconvenience of the fricking Apocalypse happening.

A knock on the door pulls my attention back to my empty room. I cross to the door and throw it open, glad for the distraction no matter who it is.

Silas stands there holding a fancily wrapped box with a half-smile on his face.

"Hello," he says, his voice sultry like silk on my skin.

I barely suppress a shiver staring into his eyes and feeling the burning passion boiling just below the surface. His magic intermingles with mine, intertwining just like our bodies could—nope, stop that line Aviella.

"Hi," I say, unsure how badly I lagged in giving an answer. He holds out the box. "What's this?"

"From Tynan," he says, watching my face.

"Of course it is," I say, rolling my eyes as I take the box and step aside letting Silas into the room. "What is it and what's it for?"

"A celebration, he asks that you wear this," Silas answers.

"Celebration? Of what? What could there possibly be to celebrate?"

"Fare from their latest trumpet hunt," Silas says.

"A trumpet hunt? You mean where he and the other dragons go out and kill whatever beasties they come across then serve them up? Gross."

"It's not wise to anger a dragon," Silas offers.

"Oh really? When are we going to get around to it's not

wise to anger me?" I ask, turning on him as I slam the box down on the table. "I don't have time to sit around here being pampered while my dad is out there being tortured or god knows what!"

"Aviella—" he starts but I cut him off.

"No!" I shout. "I've had enough of this crap, the dancing around, no one saying what they mean. It's all bullshit and I've had enough. It's time we got to work! We've been here long enough."

Silas nods, silent, waiting with interminable patience. I glare at him, anger pulsing in time with my heart. My magic warms the room, crackling with a life of its own, building to something. Then, suddenly, I feel stupid.

They are helping. I know it. No one knows what's going on any more than I do. Tynan is just being Tynan. His flair for the dramatic and extravagance is an aspect of who he is. I know him better than probably anyone else on the planet after he and two of his brothers... what? We mind-melded? Or something.

"Sorry," I sigh, flopping down in a chair.

"I understand," he says.

When I glance over, it's obvious he does. There is no animosity or hurt on his face, which is stoic and strong as ever. He motions towards the forgotten box.

"Right," I say, rising from the chair and crossing back to the table.

After opening the over-sized box, I toss the lid to one side and then pull the tissue paper aside. My breath catches in my throat. Inside is a dress that puts all the pretty finery in my wardrobe to shame. It's a stunning crimson color with purple silk accents and black lace at the neckline.

I pull it out of the box, hold it up so I can look it over. The top is a corset with a plunging neckline that I'm not sure leaves enough to cover my chest.

"Beautiful," Silas says from over my shoulder.

"Yeah," I agree.

It is, there's no arguing that. It's also revealing, extravagant, and another pointless distraction from what I should be doing. After laying it down carefully, I turn away, pushing aside the roaring desire to rip it to shreds and send it back to Tynan.

Don't piss off a dragon. Especially don't piss off one of the Horsemen of the Apocalypse who is also a dragon. Be smart, Aviella. Keep cool.

I take several deep breaths, so I can smile at Silas and shrug.

"Better?" he asks.

"Yes," I say.

"Good," he says. "You have another gift too."

"More? Ugh, does he never stop?"

"It's not from Tynan," he says, eyes boring into me.

A smile plays at the corner of my lips as, for an instant, I think he's going to make a move, finally. I've been waiting, needing, one of these sexy men to take the lead. It'd make life so much easier if they would and maybe, just maybe, this is it.

Silas reaches down, towards his pants, yes, yes this is it! Weird start, sure, but the roaring inferno of desire deep in my belly doesn't care. If he whips it out, I'll take it.

He reaches into his pocket and my heart sinks, lust making a cowardly retreat as Silas pulls something out that is in no way what my horny girl-parts were hoping to see.

He holds a delicate chain up between us and a beautiful pendant dangles, sparkling in the light. It's a design of interwoven ropes, like a Celtic knot but not quite. Tiny pieces of some kind of stones decorate where the ropes intersect causing the bright sparkles.

It's gorgeous.

"Who?" I ask.

"The mages," he says.

"Why?"

"It's from Merrick, for protection," he says.

"Protection?" I snort. "They won't hurt me."

"I know that, but the coven will feel safer knowing you have a bit more magic on your side."

"Sure, why not?" I ask, taking the delicate piece.

It gives me a soft shock when I touch it, then settles to being warm to my touch. The magic in it is very delicate, almost, I would think imperceptible. Interesting.

"Very well," Silas says, turning and walking to the door.

"You're leaving?"

"Do you need something else?" he asks, his eyes heavy with implications of those words.

If I ask, he's mine. That fact hangs between us, filling the space, making the air thick and hard to breathe. My heart races, a cold chill runs down my spine. I open my mouth, intending to say yes.

"No," my mouth betrays me.

Or rational thought. Silas nods slowly, thoughtful, then turns and silently walks out the door without another word.

Exhaling heavily, I drop back into the chair, grab the book I've been using to try and pass the time, and do my best to push away everything.

At some point I doze off while reading. The book isn't holding my attention. It's good and not its fault, but there are too many other things demanding I do something about them. Including the baser needs a woman has.

A knock at the door jerks me out of my half-doze. I wipe the sleep from my eyes and go to answer it. **Sarah** smiles and walks in without further invitation.

"I'm here to help you dress," she says.

"Oh, yeah," I say, still foggy.

She walks over to the dress where it lies spread across the table and picks it up, looking it over with a critical eye.

"Beautiful," she says. "This is going to really set you out."

"Great," I mutter. "What I never wanted."

She looks at me, barely surprised at my surliness. I guess she's getting used to me.

She moves me around and sets about getting me into the infernal contraption someone decided to call a dress. Before we're halfway into the thing, I'm fairly sure torture would be less painful.

The top is a corset which I now know is another word for not breathing. She had me inhale deeply, then exhale hard, and pulled it tight when my lungs were fully deflated. Now a deep breath is a distant memory.

As I expected this dress is way more revealing than I find actually comfortable. I've got more flesh strategically exposed than I've ever gone out in public showing.

"You are gorgeous!" she exclaims, turning me from side to side in front of the full-length mirror.

"Yeah," I agree half-heartedly.

The dress flares out at my hips, creating a wide train covered with delicate black lace flowing behind me. No matter my overall thoughts, it is beautiful.

"Did you want to wear this necklace too?" she asks, holding up the gift from Merrick.

I consider saying no. I don't need any extra protection, but it's beautiful and will accent the dress, so why not? What can it hurt, right?

"Yes," I answer.

She steps up behind me, and I hold my hair out of the way while she fastens it. When she lets it go, the pendant falls right at the top of my exposed cleavage, hanging perfectly, as if it was fitted to me.

There's a resounding knock on the door echoes through

my rooms.

"Who?" I ask, arching an eyebrow.

When I open the door, Tynan stands there dressed in the finest suit I've ever seen. Instantly, lust takes hold, and I have to tear my eyes away from him before I do something stupid.

He always looks good, as well as oozing sex, but this is more, worse, no better, no god, I don't know, but I have to get myself under control. My mouth is dry, my knees shaking, and my core is aching with pent-up need and desire.

"Beautiful," he says, the word an exhale that makes me shiver. His eyes trace over my skin leaving fire as they pass.

"Thank you," I say, barely getting the word out past the knot in my throat.

"I thought, perhaps, I could escort you to the feast?" he offers an arm, every ounce the perfect gentlemen.

"Sure," I say, glancing around the room.

I take his arm, and we walk out into the bunker that he rules. We stride in silence. It's not an uncomfortable silence, overall, which is strange in its own right. As we walk, all eyes are on us. I can feel their glares after we pass. They're jealous. If only they knew, I'd trade places with them.

Well, maybe not. I'd never be one of these glory seeking 'darlings'. That's never been, nor will it ever be my style. Maybe that's why Tynan has such an interest in me. It must get boring being surrounded by so many yes-people.

Smiling, I nod to those we pass, giving them what little I can. They may think they hate me, but they're caught in the trap. Chasing the glory of material things like hamsters on a wheel. Wanting more than they have, never satisfied, always needing the next new thing.

All I can give them is my empathy. I don't feel sorry for them, no, this is their choices. I do, though, understand and empathize with them. It's the world they know, and they're afraid to leave it.

*M*y desire burns so hot I am having trouble controlling myself. She is the most beautiful thing I've seen in lifetimes. It's more than her looks, though. Unlike the humans of my bunker, I don't get caught up in such materialistic things. No, it's her. She's a magnet, pulling me in, holding me.

The sweep of her curves in the sanguine red gown, the corset accenting her waist and hips with its corded ribbons. The ample exposure of her chest. Her eyes, those eyes could command a thousand men.

She reminds me of Helen of Troy. Though she wasn't known by that name when I knew her, and she wouldn't have been without the touch of my brothers and me. Though, in truth, there is something about this girl that puts Helen to shame.

The blushing swell of her lips holds my attention. Painted dark, those lips call to me without a word. I see an answering desire in her eyes—she feels it as I do. The only question is when. When do we give in to what we know is going to be?

I allow a smile to play across my lips. This is a game

worth playing. She is something worth having, and I want to enjoy the build up to the moment I take her.

My eyes trace the lines of her neck and shoulder, and my vision is finally drawn to the necklace hanging around her neck. I can't stop the smirk from appearing on my face.

The mages are bold to try to spy on me. It's over the top, but I will allow it, for now. I'll make sure and give their little cabal a good show. This will be amusing.

"You have other admirers," I comment, glancing at the necklace.

She places a hand over it, her cheeks coloring the most delectable shade of pink.

"Apparently," she says, her voice flat, and no emotions showing on her face besides that hint of color.

No matter the brave face, her heart rate leaps, her breathing becomes shallow, and her adrenalin spikes. She wants to hate me. I know it, but I have the same effect on her she does on me.

Our energies interact, more like magnets, pulling us together. She can't repel me any more than I can her.

"Should I be jealous?" I ask, teasing.

Her eyes widen and her mouth drops open, those full lips, oh, the things I want to do with them.

"No," she shakes her head. "Why would you?"

"Oh, Aviella," I say, shaking my head and placing my free hand over my chest. "You wound me."

She frowns, her eyes boring into mine as they narrow. "You're playing with me," she observes.

"Never," I say, grabbing her hand and raising it to my lips.

Her skin is silky soft, inviting. A micro-shiver races through her, and my body responds to that small indicator. Desire rages to life and vies for control.

Her strength is apparent and even more enticing than her

beauty, but her vulnerability is a sweet, secret center she cannot veil from me.

I drink her in, visually, for now. She is not ready for me to take, yet. It will happen, in time. She pulls her hand away from my lips.

"Enough," she snaps. Her words say no but her heart and the burning desire raging inside of her tells a different story.

"Of course, my brood await," I say, motioning ahead.

We walk to the grand hall. Two guards stand by the door, bowing as I approach. The door opens before us and the grand gala is revealed.

I've spared no expense to achieve perfection. Everyone is dressed in their finest, reminiscent of the grand French balls before the revolution. The patrons wear ornate masks, full gowns and the finest of suits.

Long tables run the length of the hall on both sides, laden with food. Two fountains mark the center point on each table, spouting chocolate into the air and catching it in a bowl at the bottom to pump it back up. An orchestra is tucked away up and to our left, the sound of the music the perfect volume to allow private conversations despite the crowds in the room.

As we enter there is a hushing gasp followed by silence. All eyes are on her, as they should be. Her discomfort is clear. She doesn't like the spotlight of their attention. Alaric and Shen look at us from the far end of the room where they stand on the raised dais, surrounded by their sycophants.

When their eyes lock on her, their desire raises the temperature in the room. Those gathered look from them to her, and back again. A slow smile spreads across my face as her heart rate increases, and blood rushes to her cheeks and neck.

It's been millennia since I've found interest in life. The problem with being a Horseman. I'm a creature of the

Supreme's Will, and for most of my existence, my actions have been guided. Now, my purpose done, I've been left to my own devices.

Will there be more for us? Are we, like some broken toy, used and tossed aside? In this long gap of time I've been left to draw my own conclusions. My brothers and I have spent many long nights discussing these matters, but to no resolution.

Looking from the celebrants to her, she is so different. What is she? More than human, but not something we've yet put our finger on.

She's not like the others gathered here, that is certain. She's more. A burning flame that calls me as if I am a moth, drawn to her. No human could have this effect on us.

Humans.

Petty, childish. What use are they who have destroyed the beautiful garden they were given?

We've never felt bad for our role in resetting the world. We knew this time would come long before they learned to string words into sentences.

Look in their hearts. They live in fear. Fear of each other, fear of the world around them. No matter how they cover it over, their pretty distractions were nothing more than a way to conceal what they truly felt. Terror that they might not be in control.

They debased themselves and in the process ruined an entire planet.

I've never seen value in them before now. Before her.

I hold out my hand and she places hers lightly in it. An electric wave blasts up my arm at the touch of her soft skin. Desire flares hot.

"Why are they all looking at me?" she asks, her voice quiet but tense.

"And why would they look at anything else? When the

sun comes out, does it not draw your eye? When you come upon a breathtaking view, do you not stop to admire it? It is what they are made to do, to appreciate true beauty."

She turns her head to me, tilting to one side as she arches an eyebrow.

"That's ridiculous," she says, rolling her eyes.

"It is most common that the truly beautiful do not see their own beauty," I say smiling.

She shakes her head and snorts.

"Your silver tongue isn't going to get you anywhere," she says but her body sends an entirely different message.

The scent of her arousal, her heart racing, a hint of musky sweat fan the flames of desire.

"Of course," I acknowledge her, smiling. "Shall we?"

I motion down the stairs with my head.

"Yes, let's get this over with," she mutters.

As we start down the stairs, the hushed voices resume conversation. I have no doubt they are talking about her. It's what I want. Let them wonder. Let them see her. She is so far above them, they cannot comprehend it.

As we walk, the most self-important of the humans comes and offers their welcome and greetings. She deals with each of them gracefully not engaging too long or encouraging them to stay.

My brothers watch our approach, reaching out to me telepathically so that they too feel the touch of her skin on mine.

"What is she?" Shen whispers in my mind.

"Beyond," Alaric answers.

"She's barely human, something more," I answer, nodding my way along with the conversations happening in front of me, giving them less than half of my attention.

"Casmir has taken note," Alaric says.

"He's pulled his attention from his puppet experiments in his locked tower?" I ask.

"Yes," Alaric answers.

"Interesting," I observe.

She moves through the shark-infested waters of the social setting with an ease and expertise that I know she's never had a chance to learn. It's natural to her, an ability that most humans spend years developing and refining.

"Perhaps it does all mean something after all," Shen says.

"What do you mean?" Alaric asks.

"The destruction they've wrought," Shen says. *"Maybe there is a reason."*

"A reason?" I ask.

"Yes, her," Shen says.

As all three of us look at Aviella and she stops mid-sentence, turning her eyes to each of us, somehow aware of our attention on her.

"See," Shen says. *"She is the key to what comes next. Whatever that is."*

A strange sensation races through my body and it takes me a moment to recognize it as anticipation of the unknown. Interesting.

CHAPTER FIVE

AVIELLA

*D*amn him.

I feel like I need a shower. Shaking hands and hobnobbing with these... people makes my skin crawl.

Still, I'm here and I do make the best I can of it. In my mind, as I meet each of these pompous fops, I imagine the antics Rowan would do making fun of them after the dinner.

"Such a pleasure to have you joining us," the man in front of me says, his voice oozing sleaze.

He's dressed in gold lame cloth suit that sparkles so much it hurts my eyes. His skin is sallow, sunken cheeks, but his eyes are a stormy grey and sparkle with intelligence. They keep darting from me to Tynan.

"Thanks," I say, ignoring his extended hand and looking past him.

"That dress," he says, his eyes drifting up and down me.

It takes all my willpower to not shudder.

"Yeah," I say, trying to be as dismissive as possible. "It's something, isn't it."

"Oh my yes," he says.

"Indeed," Tynan interjects into the conversation, his voice low with a dangerous edge to it.

The man licks his lips nervously, his tongue darting out like a snakes, then disappearing again.

"Well, my compliments," the man says, taking his leave before he further pushes his luck with Tynan.

There are, apparently, benefits to hanging with the Dragon Horseman of the Apocalypse in his home bunker.

"Is everyone here so creepy?" I mutter.

"Do you find me... creepy?" Tynan asks.

His voice is sultry, a lovers caress across my skin. His eyes passing over me with a warming gaze. My heart leaps into my throat, pounding hard in its new-found home. The fire burning low in my stomach, my lady bits tight and pounding with need, I swallow and avert my eyes from him. Why does he have this effect on me?

"No," I answer, shaking my head. "Not creepy."

"That is a relief," he says, not a hint of irony in his voice.

I look at him, fully, and study his face. He's being serious. There's nothing about Tynan that is simple. So many layers to everything he says and does.

"What is the point of all this?" I ask, meeting his eyes.

"All of what?" he asks.

"This," I motion around us. "You've got power. You could make a difference!"

"We've discussed this," he says, sighing his boredom.

"Right," I say. "Your hands are tied. Let humanity be who and what they are."

His jaw tightens as I parrot his words to him.

"In essence," he says, guiding us towards the dais where his brothers wait.

We walk up three steps, and then he leads the way around behind the long table set there. He moves to the middle seat, pulling out the chair to his left and holding it for me.

I stare at it and debate the wisdom of saying screw it and running out of here. Silas' words come back to me, though, and I can't argue that pissing off a dragon isn't a good idea, so I take the seat as gracefully as I can.

He takes his seat next to me then, to my surprise, Alaric sits to my right. Shen takes the seat on Tynan's right and they let their hangers-on take what seats they will. All three of the dragon's attention is obviously on me.

It's more than their eyes, which are constantly on me, their magic caresses my skin, interweaves with mine, enticing and intriguing.

Deep breaths. Focus. Push aside the pent-up tension and desire that's been coming on for too long.

The gathered crowds move to their respective seats around the set-up tables. The orchestral music changes, becoming softer and subtler.

Servants dressed head to toe in white file out of recessed doors carrying trays of food. The smells are delicious, almost intoxicating. My mouth waters in anticipation, until they set a plate in front of me.

I don't know what this is, or was I guess, that now lies on my plate but it not only doesn't look appetizing, it turns my stomach to look at it.

Looking askance at Tynan he smiles, nodding with an enthusiasm that doesn't appear to be feigned.

"Try it," he urges me.

"It's truly delightful," Alaric says from over my shoulder.

"You're kidding," I say.

Tynan frowns, furrowing his brow.

"Why would we 'kid' you about a delicacy?" he asks.

"It looks like it's about to get off the plate and walk away," I observe. "And that, is that it's eye?"

"It's an eye, the creature had dozens," Alaric says, not helpful.

"Oh," I say, my stomach sinking.

Laid around the... thing... are vegetables I at least recognize, and I am hungry so I pick around it, eating those things I have at least an idea of what they are.

Casting a wary eye around the room the other guests seem to be enjoying the meal immensely. It could be they're good at putting up a front though. Considering where I'm at that wouldn't be an unreasonable assumption either.

One way or the other they're eating their food with great relish. Holding up forkfuls of it with apparent delight and proclaiming its virtues.

I manage to push it, whatever it was, around long enough that the servants reappear and the dish thankfully disappears. I'm still ravenously hungry, the accent vegetables having done nothing to address my appetite.

In moments a second plate is put in front of me. This one, at least, has things that look familiar on it. Hungrily I eat everything on it.

As fast as I eat it's barely fast enough, apparently, because as soon as I lean back in my chair that plate is whisked away and yet another takes its place.

The moment I see it I almost lose everything I just ate. A tentacle lies in the center of the plate, similar to an octopus leg if it came off a giant one except where the suckers would be are tiny mouths filled with rows of razor-sharp looking teeth. Each of them open as if locked in an eternal scream.

Tearing my eyes away from it I shudder and push the plate away.

"Aviella," Tynan says. "It is extremely rude to offend the chef."

"I can't eat that," I say, refusing to even look at it.

Tynan tsks loudly and glances to one side. Following his gaze until I notice a Chinese man standing in front of one of the doors. He's dressed in white, like the ones serving dishes, but it's obvious he's not a servant. White light envelops him, coming from some unidentifiable source. He is staring directly at me, and in the bright light it's easy to see that he has no whites to his eyes. They're pure pupils, all black. He frowns deeply, a look of great displeasure on his face.

I don't know what he is, but he's not human, that I'm sure of. My magic tingles when I instinctively scan over him, but I can't get a grip on who or what he is. It's like he's slippery, my scan slips over him without revealing anything.

"Try it," Tynan says. "You'll be surprised, I assure you."

A tremor runs through my core, and my stomach roils. Picking up a tiny fork, having no idea if this is the 'proper' one to use or not, I stab into the arm thing doing my best to not look at it. Twisting and turning I tear a piece of flesh off. Breathing deep and exhaling slowly, I raise it to my lips.

Bracing myself, I close my eyes and slide it in.

Flavor explodes in my mouth like fireworks going off in my brain. It's as if every pleasure center in my brain is activated in a single stroke. I've never, in all my life, tasted anything like it.

As the flavor blooms on my tongue it changes, becoming more complex, revealing layers as I chew.

Looking over at Tynan my cheeks burn hot with embarrassment as I'm forced to nod and admit it's ridiculously good.

"Wow," I say, swallowing the piece.

"Nothing but the best, Aviella," he responds, smiling broadly. "It may not look like much but as you see the taste is out of this world."

"Literally," Alaric snorts.

I don't know if his comment makes it better or worse. Unable to decide I continue picking at and eating the trumpet fare. I don't look at it though. It's much better if I don't think about what it is I'm eating.

Four more times plates are cleared and replaced until I'm so stuffed, I'm ready for a nap.

All through the meal Alaric and Shen watch me, more than Tynan. It's not only with their eyes though, which are intrusive enough, they're magic caresses. Reaching, touching, retreating, never going far. It's a strange, mystical, unseen game of cat and mouse. They reach and they withdraw.

It wouldn't be so bad if it wasn't so damn arousing. Some part of me, that I barely want to admit to, likes it. Their attention is an intoxicating, heady spirit that calls to something deep and primal.

It's charged with fire, an electrical hum that promises pleasures unknown to mortal kind. No matter all my 'world-saving' responsibility, I've got needs and they're calling to them. Pulling, teasing, making it harder and harder to resist.

Tynan rises to his feet, pushing his chair back. Rising myself he pulls my chair out then offers me his hand.

"May I have this dance?" he asks.

Suddenly, I'm the little orphan girl abandoned to the system. There were dances organized then, arranged affairs to force us to socialize, and they were the worst. No one ever wanted to dance with me. I was the weird girl, the one with no friends, strange and not safe.

Except now I'm being picked.

By, literally, the most popular man in the room, barring his brothers who might compete, but this is his bunker.

Stumbling over my own thoughts, I can't form the words to say yes, so I nod mutely and take his hand. He helps me to my feet and together we walk around the table and down the dais.

As if on some silent command only they can hear the area is clear but all eyes are on us. Only now, as we step out onto the floor, does it hit me I can't dance.

"Tynan, I... can't dance," I whisper, an urgency to my voice as I try to come up with a way out of the nightmare I've walked myself into.

"Follow my lead," he says. "You'll do fine."

"We've got you," Shen says, appearing to one side.

"Trust us," Alaric says.

Their magic flows against me with a soothing melody that calms my nerves. Inhaling I nod. Tynan holds his right arm out to the side while placing his left on my waist.

Uncertainly I place my hand in his and rest my free hand on his shoulder. His smile is dazzling as his eyes bore into me, oozing sexual tension and energy.

On cue, the orchestra strikes a chord as one unit, violins taking the lead with a staccato rhythm. He moves us quickly to one side, our arms leading the charge as if we're racing over the ramparts in some fierce battle.

I'm swept along with him, following his lead with an ease that belies my lack of skill. I'm dimly aware of Alaric and Shen moving with us but as they move they make shapes with their arms, one over their head, the other in front, as if forming boxes around their torsos. Our legs move from side to side and I'm proud that I barely stumble as he guides me.

Flowing from one end of the dance floor to the other, our bodies pressing closely together, so close his energy engulfs me. His heart beats against my chest and his arousal is unmistakable through his trousers as it digs into my stomach.

We move with a fluidity I'd never accomplish on my own and my heart soars as we do.

Suddenly he stops, twisting my hand lightly and I flow along with the implied motion, spinning in place as he extends his arm. My spin comes to a stop as both our arms are outstretched fully, hands clasping each other. Alaric and Shen close with me then, pressing their bodies hard against mine from either side.

Light-headed, I struggle to remain upright, but the press of their bodies won't let me fall even if I do pass out. They grind against me, their hands moving up and down my sides while Tynan holds my eyes locked to his with some entrancing power.

The world around us is forgotten. There are only the four of us. Pulsing, pounding bodies filled with primal needs and desires. I could care less as the fleeting thought of being watched during such intimacy occurs to me.

The dragon's allure is a soft, taunting fire. Warming more than my skin. Alaric and Shen step off of me and Tynan is there, holding firm as he guides me across the dance floor. They could undress me, and I don't think I'd balk. Thinking of it, I wonder, briefly, if the witches' amulet is holding their seductive natures at bay at all. If so, I can't tell. They're too enticing.

Let them watch. I need this. Need them. Need to be taken, but more I need to take what is mine. What they offer to me, so freely.

CHAPTER SIX

TYNAN

'*She's extraordinary*,' Shen says on the telepathic connect my brothers and I share.

'Not the average specimen, by a long shot,' Alaric contributes.

'I said as much,' I remind them.

'You've hogged her too long to yourself,' Alaric says.

'Have I not shared her?' I ask.

'Barely,' Shen says, stepping in close to Aviella, his hand on her waist, taking her hand and spinning her in to him then twirling her out where Alaric expertly takes her into his waiting arms.

'She is a rare, sweet fruit,' Alaric says.

Even his telepathic voice is heavy with lust and desire. His body presses hard against hers, pinning her once more between Shen and himself as they grind.

My cock throbs as her desire flashes white hot, washing over the three of us with the force of a tidal wave.

'It's easy to see why the Shadow Factions want her dead,' Shen says, his eyes closing, his head leaning back with pleasure. 'Her power is delectable.'

The music plays on and we move her between us, guiding her around the dance floor. The sycophants watch, their jealousy filling the space, any one of them would kill or worse to have our attention like this for mere seconds.

She isn't like them. She rejects us no matter how much she wants us. It only makes her that much more interesting.

'She is the key,' Alaric says.

'Do you think?' I ask, taking her hand and moving her with quick, steady steps across the floor in perfect time with the beat of the song playing.

'Yes,' Alaric says, his eyes catching mine as I turn with her then hand her off to Shen. 'The fragments we've found so far indicate that she is it. She will lead us to our purpose.'

Purpose. Such a simple word, so many implications. Since our 'job' finished after we played our role in the Apocalypse, it's what we've been sorely lacking.

'She's going to be our freedom,' Shen says, stalking the dance floor with her, every bit the hunter.

'That could be,' I say.

He guides her in close, Shen and I surround her with him. One girl between the three of us but if any woman could take us all, it is Aviella.

She is beautiful. Shining with a majestic, golden light as she flows with us, fluid as if she has been dancing since the day she was born.

We press into her, melding our bodies against hers. Her heart races, her skin is flushed, desire rolls off of her. Her touches linger on each of us as we pass her one to another.

Her magic crackles with life, alive with desire. It pulls us in, washes away the world around us. She is the all.

Suddenly she steps out of Alaric's arms.

"I... have to go," she says, biting her lip and shaking her head.

Before any of us can say a word she turns and walks

quickly out of the room. A soft gasp comes from the watchers.

"Music!" I say, loudly and the band starts a fresh song.

We don't say anything to each other, the three of us take off after her.

She deflects our probes easily, as if without conscious thought. Following as she speed walks down the hall it's clear the desire is getting to her but why she ran is not.

"Aviella," I call.

She hesitates before stopping and turning.

"What?" she snaps.

"What indeed?" I ask.

She flushes brightly, biting her lower lip. At last she closes her eyes and shakes her head.

"I can't do this," she whispers.

I nod, understanding, Alaric and Shen do as well. We're drawn to her and it's far more than her beauty that pulls us in.

'You feel it?' Alaric asks.

'She is gravity, our destiny is tied to hers,' Shen says.

It's true. There is no mistaking the pull she has on all of us.

"Why? Why me? Why any of this?" She throws her hands up and looks around. "You're Dragons!"

A shockwave runs through each of us, echoing across our telepathic connection.

"That is an astute question," I say, reaching for her hand but she pulls it back before I can take it.

"Sure, how about an actual answer?" she arches an eyebrow and places a hand on her hip.

Looking askance at my brethren they each, in turn, nod.

"You," I say, simple and direct.

"That's not an answer!" she says, her voice rising. "I'm a girl, I get it, big destiny, all that jazz. I'm barely coming to terms with it but you... the three of you. You're so much more. You're the freaking Horsemen!

What's the connection between us? Why do I feel so damn drawn to you?"

"We have the same question," I say. "Our purpose has been served, we've heralded the Apocalypse as we were guided to do. Since, we have been on our own. It seems our fate is tied to you."

She shakes her head.

"I can't deal with this, not you too," she whispers.

Her words carry a weight and instinctively we, as one, probe towards her thoughts. The probe slides across a shield without penetrating and she seems to be unaware of the attempt.

Shen and Alaric frown and we push in again.

"Oh, there you are," Silas says, interrupting us.

My brethren and I glare at him, but Aviella turns towards him gratefully.

"Silas," I say, "we are in the middle of a--"

"I'm so glad to see you!" Aviella exclaims, cutting off my admonishment.

Silas smiles, his cool eyes locking with mine. There is no doubt as to his timing or his intentions.

"We were going to do some new experiments," he says, accepting her embrace if stiffly.

"Right," she says, the barest of hesitations in the word. "Sorry Tynan, I have to go."

"Of course," I say, maintaining a cool exterior while inside I struggle to control raging desire and the urge to turn Silas to ash then have my way with her.

Silas nods and leads her away. They move quickly out of our sight, leaving the three of us alone.

"The Methuselah plays a dangerous game," Alaric growls.

"We could change the rules," Shen says in a soft, dangerous tone.

"No," I say, shutting them down. "We are in control, always. Let the game play out, for now."

The scent of her lingers on the air and I inhale it deeply dreaming of the time that I will, eventually, make her mine.

CHAPTER SEVEN

AVIELLA

*S*ilas leads the way to my chambers in stoic silence. I appreciate him not questioning me about Tynan and the dragons. I don't know what I would or could say.

He waits for me to let us in then, businesslike, he asks me to stand with my arms out to either side. He passes a metal wand of some kind over and around me. He keeps his attention on what he's doing but I feel him. Magic creates an energy field around each of us that I'm becoming increasingly aware of and as his mingles with mine I sense his tension.

He's struggling to control himself. I'm not sure what, but I think, or maybe I hope, it's desire. Desire for me, like I feel for him.

Damn it, the dragons have me all worked up again. It's the worst part of being around them, they call out my most primal nature. Desire is a burning furnace inside of me and sooner or later I've got to give in.

"Interesting," Silas says, looking at the wand.

"Yeah?" I ask, looking for anything to distract me. Silas nods, frowning at the wand but doesn't say more. "That is?"

He looks up at my prompting and for a clear moment it's as if he's surprised I'm here. Rolling my eyes at him I nod to encourage him to actually speak.

"Oh," he says, shaking his head. "Sorry. This is a puzzle."

"This being me?" I ask, a sense of righteous indignation rising.

"Yes," he says, focused on the wand.

"Great," I say, full on sarcasm.

He looks up again with surprise clear on his face. It seems to register, for the first time, with him what he's said and how it sounds.

"Sorry," he says, sighing. "It's, I'm trying to help."

"I know," I say, my voice soft, reaching out I touch his chest.

It's electric, our magic suddenly meets and both repels and pulls at the same time. Static shock sparkles where I touched his chest and both of our breaths hitch as we look at each other.

My cheeks warm as blood rushes to them and to much lower places adding even more fuel to my desire.

"Aviella," he says, his voice low and husky.

I can't form words so I nod. The auras of our magic mixes, caressing each other while our bodies stay locked on that single, simple contact.

"Yes," I say.

A simple word that says so much more. Yes, say more. Yes, tell me. Yes, take me. Please, take the decision out of my hands and take me.

"Not like this," he says, a steel curtain falling in his eyes.

Disappointment fills me and I can't even begin to hide it.

"Right," I say, nodding. "Smart."

And it is right and it is smart but that doesn't change any of the facts. I want him.

"You are--" he stops himself, shakes his head, then says

something I'm sure is completely different than what he started out with. "My greatest puzzle. Your lineage is ancient, we knew that, this wand gives some clues as to your ancestral lines. I'll turn it over to the mages and see if they can find anything more."

"Good," I say, taking my hand off his chest.

Cold settles on me as I straighten my shoulders and force myself to swallow.

"I should go," he says.

"Okay," I agree. "I'll see you later."

Silently he leaves the room, and I'm alone, again. Hot, bothered, and alone, despite having almost a dozen men, all of which I'm certain want me, and any one of which would be an amazing lover, I'm alone.

"Gah!" I exclaim to the empty room.

Nervous energy bubbles through me and I need to do something. Anything.

Focusing my magic I form it into a shield around me then let that go. Okay, what now? That killed all of two seconds.

Pacing the room I count the steps wall-to-wall several times to give my mind something to focus on besides the way my body is feeling.

"So many men," I say out loud. "And I can't choose. Why can't I choose?"

Pacing I answer myself.

"Because you're greedy," I observe.

It's true. I am, but not greedy in a sex-obsessed way, I'm not that girl. No, I'm greedy in that I value each and every one of them. They're each special to me, and I don't want to hurt any of them.

I don't need magic to know they want me. All of them do, even if they're not all as open about it as Tynan and his brothers are. Those three... a shudder races down my spine. Yeah, well, that's that, isn't it?

48

If I sleep with one of them though, any one of them, the others would be hurt. Even imagining it, my stomach hurts, and tears form in the corners of my eyes. How could I hurt them like that?

"Dad," I whisper. "What do I do?"

He doesn't answer. That's good. Dad and I were close, really close, but I don't think I could have a talk with my dad about which man to choose as a lover. That would be awkward.

A knock at the door finally interrupts the downward spiral of my thoughts, and I bound over to answer it, thankful for the interruption.

Maybe it's Tynan, come to make my choice for me.

Efram's eyes widen in surprise, and he smiles easily.

"Wow, that was fast, were you leaving?" he asks.

"No, come in!" I exclaim, excited that he's here.

He walks in, eyes roaming over me. Only then do I realize I'm still dressed for Tynan's ball, makeup and all.

"You look... gorgeous," he says, admiration flowing through his magic.

My cheeks warm at his compliment and I nod, suddenly feeling shy.

"Thank you," I say.

We stare at each other for a moment that stretches just to the point of being awkward. Underneath the tension with Efram, my skin thrums with the memory of Tynan, Shen, and Alaric's touch. Efram, my oldest friend, the one whom I've had the longest interest in... I could.

Except the ball has been in his court for a long time, and I'm still waiting. Do I take it back and run with it?

His eyes drop to my exposed chest. Warmth flushes my cleavage a soft pink until his eyes lock on to the necklace around my neck. "Is that from Merrick?" he asks.

I look down, flustered, grab it and lift it up. "This? Yeah," I say.

He grimaces and nods. "What did he tell you?" he asks.

"Silas brought it, said it was for protection," I say, frowning. "Why?"

Efram smiles and shakes his head.

"The witches are playing a dangerous game," he says. "There's a scrying spell embedded into it. They were trying to ascertain information."

Things suddenly click into place. The way Tynan looked at it and smiled, getting the gift, Silas showing up right when he did. My anger flickers, but I can't muster the energy for it.

They're struggling to survive, like the rest of us. I'm fine with that, but they need to damn well know I'm not going to be a pawn in their games. They want my help, they need to be open and honest with me.

"Damn it," I curse, my anger overriding and pushing aside the sexual tension between us. "I'm going to give them a piece of my mind."

Decision made and a course of action before me, I set into motion. I unclasp the dress, then struggle to reach the zipper.

"Argh, can you?" I ask, looking at Efram.

His eyes widen the slightest bit, his lips purse, then he nods stiffly. He takes the zipper and lowers it, exposing the skin of my back.

I'm not wearing a bra because the dress has built-in support. My breasts drop as the pressure holding them up releases. Cool air hits the exposed skin of my back as the dress unzips to the lowest part of my back. His eyes roam up and down the curve of my spine.

Openly teasing now, I wriggle my hips to work the dress a bit more free and then slide it down and off, exposing my bare ass. He stiffens more than physically, his magic pulls away from me, becoming stuffy and stoic.

He forces his eyes up to mine, and I meet his gaze over my shoulder, openly defiant. Daring him to take what I'm offering.

He doesn't lower his gaze even an inch. If I couldn't feel his desire as if it's an inferno blasting out waves of heat, I'd feel ashamed—but I do.

"Aviella," he says, his voice flat.

Ignoring him, I walk over to a water basin, grab a cloth, and wash the makeup off my face.

Openly daring him to say or do... anything. Please.

Ever the perfect gentleman, no matter how much I wish he wouldn't be, he turns around to give me a modicum of privacy.

Oh Efram, I sigh internally. He treats me like I'm a holy relic. One of these men is going to claim me, and damn it, I'm ready to be taken.

"Any word yet on Nathaniel or Rafe?" I ask, pulling on a pair of jeans and a sweatshirt.

"No," he says. "Nothing new since we last spoke."

"Okay," I say. "Let's go."

"Go?" he asks, turning around in surprise.

His eyes take in my now-dressed state, and regret mixed with relief passes over his face.

"Yes, go," I say, motioning towards the door.

"Where are we going?" he asks.

"I'm going to give Merrick a piece of my mind," I state flatly. He opens his mouth to argue, but I hold up a single finger between us. "No. I'm done with this. I'm not a pawn in anyone's game."

He frowns, then nods, and we walk out into the bunker, heading for the lower levels where the witches have their hideout. We walk in silence while I fume, anger growing with each step. So many things in my life I don't have any control over, but this one thing I'm going to put a stop to.

Merrick can play whatever games he wants against the dragons, but not using me.

I'm not sure what the dragons intend, and I definitely don't agree with a lot of what they do, but I trust them. Mostly. Our goals align, which is more than I can say for Merrick. The tunnels are filled with the half-starved sycophants putting themselves on display. It turns my stomach looking at them. Their gaunt frames, scars on their arms from self-mutilation, sunken, dull eyes—they look awful, but this is the new standard of beauty, for this bunker at least.

I almost turn back, looking at all of them. After all, no matter what he says to the contrary, Tynan is in charge here. If he said something, things would change, I'm sure of it. Next time I see him, I'm going to tell him to fix this in no uncertain terms, but that doesn't change what Merrick did. It's high time I take some control back over my life, so we continue on our way.

When we get to the witches hideout, several of them try to stop my entrance, but a soft word from Efram, and they step aside, though they give me some dark looks.

Let them look.

Merrick walks out to meet us with four witches flanking him, three males and a female. How many witches are in his coven?

"How was the ball?" Merrick asks, with only the barest hint of sarcasm.

"Who do you think you are?" I ask, glaring.

"I'm not sure I understand the question," he says.

I throw the necklace at him. His hand darts out with surprisingly quick reflexes and catches it mid-air. He holds it up in between us, letting it sparkle.

"That," I say, spitting the word. "Protection? Really? I trusted you."

"I see," he says, looking the pendant a moment then, handing it to the witch on his left.

"You see? That's it?" I ask, hands on hips, feeling righteously indignant.

"Yes," he nods. "Was there anything else?"

This isn't going at all the way I had played it out in my head. Confusion creates frustration, and with him not responding to my anger with something like anger in return I don't know what I want out of this.

"Yes," I say, defiantly pushing on. "I'm not your pawn. Don't lie to me and don't ever try to use me again."

"Okay," he says.

Staring at him, seething with unexpressed rage, I throw my hands up in the air.

"What is your game? What are you trying to do here?" I ask.

"Hide," he says. "I apologize for not telling you about the scrying spell. I was hoping to garner information on the Dragon's next move."

"Did you like what you saw?" I ask, feeling bitter as I think about that dance with all three of them. The invasion of my privacy. Merrick seeing how they... my cheeks burn hot as I shut down that line of thought.

"It didn't cut through their shields," he says, his voice deadpan but something in his eyes tells me there is more that he's not saying. He knows.

Reaching out with my magic, I want to ascertain what he knows and what he doesn't. There's something he's not telling me, of that I'm certain.

Pressing forward my magic hits a barrier like running into a wall. I can't push past it. A solid force. Locking eyes with Merrick I press harder, trying to force my way through but it doesn't budge. Stretching my senses out I look for a way around it but this entire area is warded. Merrick nods as I withdraw.

"We have no ulterior motives, Aviella," he says. "We're trying to survive and protect our own. That is all."

"That's fine, but don't use me. If you need my help, ask."

"Would you have?" he asks, tilting his head to one side.

"Yes," I say, too quick then I think about it. "Maybe. I'd certainly listen to your case and reason for needing my help."

"Fair enough," he says, nodding.

"All right, well not again, okay?"

"I agree," he says, his voice solemn.

Efram silently watches the exchange between the two of us. Merrick and I stare at each other for a long moment then we both nod as if on some external cue.

Spinning on my heel, I storm out and head back home, Efram trailing in my wake. I don't say anything until we're back at my door. I throw it open and walk in, but Efram stops in the doorway.

"Better?" Efram asks.

"Yes," I say, then shake my head. "No. Ugh, this all sucks."

"It does," Efram says, lowering his voice so I can barely hear him. "They'll be back soon, and then we'll know what our next move is."

"Good. I'm tired of waiting," I say. "Patience has never been a virtue of mine."

"I never would have guessed that," he smiles. "Good night, Aviella. Sleep well."

"You don't have to go," I say, impulsively throwing the offer out.

He stops mid-turn, looking over his shoulder. Delight sparkles in his eyes for an instant, then his jaw tightens and he shakes his head.

"I know," he says, his voice thick and husky. "It's for the best."

"Right," I say, unable to keep the disappointment from my voice.

He hesitates another long moment and I think, for an instant of it, that he's going to throw caution to the wind. His hand clenches and he shakes his head once more stepping out of my doorway and shutting it behind himself.

It closes with a loud click and a finality that makes me feel more alone than any time since my Dad left me on my own.

I go to my bathroom and wash my face. Cold water does nothing to quench the thirst of my desires or wash away the empty loneliness. Plopping into an overstuffed chair, I take up one of the romance novels stacked by it and start reading. It's another reverse harem story, and as I turn the pages, ideas and fantasies play out in my head.

Impossible, unreal fantasies, that would never work in the real world.

Would they?

No, get a grip girl. This is not the world I live in even if it is the Apocalypse. No matter how enticing it seems.

A knock at the door jerks me out of my reading and I leap to my feet, almost glad for a distraction from my distraction.

CHAPTER EIGHT

TYNAN

*S*eeing my guests off was easy, slipping away from Shen and Alaric was more difficult. My brothers are crude, and I'm certain they scared Aviella. It's the only thing that makes sense. Her desire was unmistakable.

She is refined fruit, no matter her humble origin. She is so much more than a conquest in some eternal, boring game, to be marked in a century long one-upping.

Only when I confronted them with their overpowering energy did they finally agree to let me go to her alone and even then, they were reluctant.

She draws us to her. Our fates, somehow, are intertwined with hers. It's fascinating. All these years, waiting, being activated when the will of the Divine saw fit.

Activated. Shaking my head, I cringe, mentally, at the thought. None of them understand: when we are called, we have no choice. The mantle of Horsemen isn't light, laying over and overriding our natures as dragons even.

We've each of us learned to cope with it in our own ways. Shen and Alaric compete incessantly with each other. Casmir has been obsessed for years with humanity and his puppet making, locking himself away for decades to do his experiments. I've amused myself in various ways.

So many years have passed we've become numb to most everything, but she sparks desires and thoughts of freedom. Ones I thought long lost to the mists of time.

Stopping at her door I gather my thoughts before knocking. The moment I do something clatters inside the room then her footsteps sound. Her heartbeat is loud in my ears and the scent of her drifts through the door, enticing my senses. She opens the door and my breath catches.

She is beautiful.

Her eyes widen, her mouth parts, perfect full lips glistening as if in invitation. Her heart rate increases, and she trembles ever so slightly.

"Hello," I say.

"Tynan," she says, not moving, her voice soft as the finest of silks. It brushes across my skin as does her magic, softly caressing.

"May I come in?" I ask, arching an eyebrow and giving her a half-smile.

"Huh, oh, of course," she says, stepping to one side.

She's changed from her finery into plain clothing. Her preference, obviously, since I have gone to lengths to ensure her wardrobe is filled with choices of a much finer nature.

As I walk in I brush against her, the slightest of touches, but the response in her body ignites all my barely suppressed passions.

Forcing my desire under control by will alone, I stop in the middle of her rooms, turning to her and smiling, taking care nothing breaks my facade.

She seems flustered. Confusion in her eyes, no matter how she tries to hide it from her face. Her magical energy is erratic, reaching for me and withdrawing at the same time.

"Thank you," I say, carefully letting her have time to regain her composure.

"Sure," she says, shaking her head, then the all-too-familiar steel sets into her eyes. "Why are you here?"

She cocks her head oh-so-slightly to one side exposing the delicate line of her neck under her hair. Tracing it with my eyes down, across her shoulder, down to the swell of her breasts distracts me for a moment too long. She taps her foot, impatient for my answer.

"To apologize," I say.

Her mouth opens, and she furrows her brow.

"Apologize?" she asks.

"Yes," I smile. "My brothers were overly forward. I do not want you thinking less of us."

"Thinking less of you," she repeats staring.

"Yes, my beautiful parrot," I tease.

She shakes her head, and inhales deeply.

"I assure you that their behavior has nothing to do with why I might think less of you," she snaps, pushing past me and taking a seat.

Following her lead, I take a seat across from her. Close, but not too close.

"Oh?" I prompt.

She frowns. "I've already told you how I feel about this place. The way these people are, starving themselves for your amusement. Putting themselves on display, their petty, stupid games of one upping each other."

"You have," I agree. "As I recall, though, I countered that it is not of our doing."

"You could change it!" she says, leaning forward.

Her eyes are alight with a fire of indignation and injustice. Her magic slams against me, a physical distraction that enflames desire in my loins and in my heart.

How can she care so much? Her fury is self-righteous. I

wish I could feel it for myself, I drink it in. I'm not sure I've ever felt such depths of emotions. If I did, the memories of it are lost to time.

"They're suffering!" she yells, rising to her feet, hands waving in the air. "You do nothing and they suffer."

"It is their society," I say, leaning back into the chair. "Not ours."

"You have the power to change it," she says, glaring.

"Why would I?" I ask.

The look on her face moves from indignation to disbelief. She shakes her head, not taking her eyes off of mine.

"Why?" she asks. "Are you serious? You are, you're not kidding. Because it's the right thing to do!"

"By whose standards?" I counter.

"Right isn't by someone's standards, it's right. Don't try to equivocate morality with me!"

"Okay," I say, holding my hands up in surrender.

"Okay?" she says.

The fire burning in her heart is an inferno that causes her magic to flare. The warmth washes over me, a wave of energy fueled by her anger, but beneath the anger lies desire. Her heart is racing, loud in my ears.

Rising to my feet, I close into her space, grabbing her by her waist. Her head raises, mouth opens, and I expect her to protest, but then her lips smash into mine forcefully, her tongue pushing into my mouth.

I pull her tight against me, my erection digging into her stomach. All semblance of control is gone. I must have her.

Her hands wrap around my neck, twining in my hair. She tugs me down into her. Grabbing her ass, I lift and she wraps her legs around my waist.

She tears at my shirt, the buttons giving way easily. Her magic swirls around us, tingling against my skin, enhancing every sense.

My magic mingles with hers, intertwining as soon our bodies will.

She attacks me, driving her hands down between us and under my pants. No waiting. She moans loud into our kiss as her hand touches the head of my cock.

Pleasure so intense rocks through me, I almost explode. Nothing, in all my life has felt like her simple touch.

Keeping one hand under her ass, I grab her t-shirt at the neck and rip, using the slightest touch of magic so that it rips straight down exposing her bare breasts.

Groaning I move towards the bedroom, not taking my mouth from hers. Our tongues wrestle, vying for dominance. The heat between us rises and her heart pounds in my ears.

She drops her legs from my waist, stopping my motion to the bedroom as she puts her feet back on the ground. Sliding down me, her breasts dragging across my abs, she lowers herself to her knees in front of me.

She struggles for a moment with my pants, so I help her, needing her more than I've ever needed or wanted anything.

My stiff dick flops out, erect before her and she doesn't hesitate, grabbing and stroking it while teasing the head with her tongue and mouth.

"Aviella," I moan.

She groans then slides my dick down and into her throat. My balls tighten. She works it hard and fast, furiously pushing me to the edge but I'm not interested in taking my pleasure, I want to explore her.

Grabbing her shoulders, I pull her up. She resists, so I exert a bit of magic and she rises off the floor and I sweep her into my arms.

Racing into the bedroom I lay her out on the bed, ripping her pants in my hurry to free her of them.

Pausing, for a moment, I admire her perfection.

She is beautiful, every aspect of her is as if drawn by an artist.

She bites her lower lip, eyes downcast, and her cheeks and breasts flush a delicate pink.

Moving the fingers of my left hand I manipulate magic, letting a soft current of it flow across her skin, enticing and exciting her. As it obeys my will I lower myself between her legs, ready to explore her delicate flower.

Closing with her mound she shivers so I slow, kissing my way up her left thigh. Keeping the magic flowing across and around her it is but a thought to have it teasing her nipples then forming it into a solid I penetrate her waiting pussy at the same time I open her folds with my tongue.

The sweet, heavenly taste of her is everything I imagined. It's more.

She moans, soft at first, but growing louder as I explore, finding every fold and making sure every bit of her is given my full attention.

My magic gives me more hands, giving her pleasure across her body.

She groans, then bucks against me, grabbing me by my hair and pulling me tight against her hot, wet pussy. I flatten my tongue against her slick clit while pushing the solid cylinder of magic deep into her.

With a thought, both her nipples are teased by magic, then an orgasm rocks through her. Her back arches, toes curl, and her hands tighten in my hair, holding me in close.

She doesn't even breathe as it rolls through her body until the first wave of it passes, and she's groaning as she pants.

My cock throbs with desire.

Experiencing her like this is pleasure beyond anything. As her body relaxes, quivering as the last waves of the orgasm grip and release her, she looks up and licks her lips.

"Fill me," she orders.

An order I'll gladly obey. One I don't think I could resist if I wanted to.

She rolls over, presenting her heart-shaped ass to me with her knees bent and pushing it back into me. My cock slides into her ready pussy with surprising ease.

Her body welcomes me, accepting my girth, gripping my dick like a glove.

"Yes!" her screams muffled by the comforter of the bed.

I drive into her, forcing her forward then she rocks back into me. We push and pull, in and out, building the pleasure.

Her hands knot into the sheets, gripping and releasing in time with my thrusts.

Holding her by her hips I drive in deeper, pushing her further forward each time. Slapping the swell of her ass, delighting in the way it turns pink, I pound her with my need.

Desire is all. Control is not something I relinquish ever, but in this case I'm at the mercy of my desire and her.

"Yes, yes, yes," she grunts with each thrust, and I answer her with my own grunts of pleasure.

My dick swells, my balls tighten, and I'm so close. Dancing on the edge, I hold off my release until I feel her body responding in kind.

She grows warmer, her magic is a fire roaring against me. Sliding my hands along her sides, up and over her ass, I thrust faster.

Close. So close. No holding back.

Her pussy contracts on my dick, and I'm over the edge. My dick spasms, stars fills my vision, her magic washes through me, blasting away my inherent shields and protection.

I'm burned to a cinder in the white-hot flash of her. Washing away all that I was.

As awareness of the world slowly returns, I'm holding her

tight against me, feeling her body shiver and contort as the last of her pleasure finishes.

As I slide out of her she rolls over and sprawls across the bed, a half-smile on her face.

"I needed that," she exhales.

Lying down next to her she shifts and puts her head on my chest.

Her power, expended during our lovemaking, refills. I sense it flowing into her but it's different. Something has changed. She shivers then rises onto an elbow and looks around the room.

"What is it?" I ask.

"I don't know," she says. "Something has changed, I can't put a finger on what."

Nodding, post-sex exhaustion settling over me I reach out with my own magic, trying to sense what she is missing.

My magic flows.

No, it always flows, but this is... different. Focusing I reach out with my senses and nothing stops them. A barrier, one I've had so long it was normal, is gone.

I sit straight up, testing the sensation. It is true, there can be no doubt.

"What?" she asks me now in her turn.

"My curse," I say, even my voice sounding strange in my ears.

"Your curse?" she asks, arching an eyebrow.

"The mark, it's gone," I say, looking at her in wonder.

"I'm not tracking what you're saying," she shakes her head.

"I wasn't always a horseman, it was a curse, a mark laid on my brothers and me. It's... it's gone."

CHAPTER NINE

AVIELLA

*S*omething has changed.

What, I don't know, but something. Waking up, my eyes are dry and burning. Walking into the bathroom I'm dizzy and light-headed.

After Tynan left last night I fell asleep almost immediately. Satisfied after my long dry spell. I slept deeply and for the first time in recent memory I don't recall any strange dreams.

I run some water into the sink, splash it on my face, then look in the mirror.

"What in the..." I trail off, staring at my eyes. They're bloodshot. Red, swollen and veiny.

"I look like I was on the world's worst bender," I comment to myself.

I rub them and splash more water, but nothing is helping. The burning continues. I didn't even drink last night, what the hell. Sighing, I turn on the shower and let it warm up. When there's a good steam billowing out to fill the room I step in, letting the warm water wake me up.

As my skin flushes with the warmth, my heart starts

racing, and then suddenly, my veins feel like they're on fire. Molten lava pumping through them with each beat of my heart.

Crying in pain, I can't turn the water cold fast enough, shutting the hot completely off. Once there's nothing but cold flowing, the pain eases, and then it passes as if nothing happened.

There's a tingling sensation, and my magic surges in waves, rising and falling of its own accord.

Anger hits me out of nowhere. Unreasonable, irrational anger. I want to hit something, someone. Anyone. It doesn't matter who. Power races through me as I walk out of the shower dripping wet but not bothering to dry.

When I enter the sitting room area of my quarters, the magic explodes, and waves of force burst through the room. Objects fly before the blast, glass shattering, and solid objects being driven into the walls.

Crying out, I drop to my knees, unable to contain the emotions or the magic.

Kneeling, panting, I let it pass, until at last I feel under control. I get up and look around. The room is wrecked. I go to the bedroom and dress, still shaking, then sit on the edge of the bed.

"What is this?" I whisper, looking at my hands.

Power courses through my veins. Pure, raw power. It's more than I've ever felt before.

My magic has always been strange, and it's definitely been growing stronger as I come to understand it, but this is something entirely new, different, and out of the norm.

It's like I leveled up, but it came with some hidden drawbacks. I'm not in control, for one.

I close my eyes and focus on my breathing. I listen to my heartbeat until it slows and I'm calm. The quiet of the room is peaceful, so I focus on that.

As I do, I become aware of Tynan. It's not scrying exactly. I know where he is, approximately. He's angry, really angry, fighting with his brothers. They're arguing.

I can't hear it, it's not like that, but it is a certainty. I know. I don't know how but I do.

"No," I mutter, opening my eyes, swallowing hard. "It can't be..."

What have I done?

I close my eyes and visualize my magic the way Silas and Efram have taught me. Seeing it with my mind's eye, surging energy I control, a dynamo of power inside of me. Today, it's brighter than ever.

The power of it flows out, an aura that surrounds me, interacting with the environment. As I look with my mind's eye I see a thread that runs off from me, through the wall and away. There, that thread is the source.

I know exactly where it leads.

"Oh shit," I exhale hard, stomach flinching and tightening as if I've been punched. "That's not going to be easy to hide."

Shaking, I stand up and pace the room, trying to think through the ramifications. I've worried about this so much, certain that if I take any one of the boys as a lover then the others would get mad and leave.

Tears well up and I can't hold them back, thinking about losing any one of them. I've screwed it all up. Acting on impulse and rolling with the moment.

Tynan oozes sex, it was so primal, and I was so damn ready. Will they understand? How do I fix this?

Anger blazes, but this time, as it does I notice the thread connecting Tynan and me pulses with a life of its own. It's *his* anger, *his* impulsiveness feeding into me, mingling with my own.

"Oh Aviella, what have you done?"

There's nothing to do for it then. It is what it is and now

I'll have to navigate my way through the fallout. My resolve hardens, and to some degree, I'm ready to confront what's next. Whatever that is.

Splashing water on my face and trying to get rid of the puffiness from the tears, I stare at myself in the mirror.

"Okay, you're a big girl. You got this."

My eyes are still bloodshot, but there's nothing I can do about that. Nodding in self-affirmation, I smile, not really feeling it but might as well do my best.

The best thing to do with something you don't want to do is get it over with, my Dad used to tell me. Right, that's what I'm going to do.

Who first? Silas or Efram?

Oh Efram. Everything freezes as I think of my dear, tender friend. He'll take it the hardest. He's so stoic and there's no denying how much he wants me or how much of a perfect gentlemen he's always been.

Maybe I don't say anything, maybe, if I push him, we could...

There's a knock at the door interrupting my crazy thoughts. As I walk to it I try not to acknowledge how glad I am for the interruption. Hurting Efram would be the worst.

"Hello?" I ask, staring at a ridiculously scrawny young boy, I think, who is leaning against my doorframe.

"You're invited," he says, his voice soft and sing-songy.

"Invited to what?" I ask, my hackles rising. An over-whelming urge to bite his head off almost wins out but I suppress that before it exits my mouth.

"A tournament, special for you," he says, a wry grin on his face. He holds ups his arms, which look like two twigs, and flourishes with them, but I can't help noticing the multitude of scars on them.

"Great," I growl. "I don't have time for this."

"What?" he asks, eyes wide and mouth dropping open.

"I said I don't have time for this, tell Tynan to piss off," I say.

"But... you... I..." He's shaking like a leaf, tossing his head wildly side-to-side.

"You what?" I ask.

I want him to cower before me. I want to smell his fear. I want to feel his submission.

His mouth moves, but no words come out. He takes a step back, and I move with him, closing the space between us.

"Lord Tynan," he sputters. "You..."

"You what?" I ask.

What the hell am I doing? Stepping back I close my eyes and regain control of myself. Obviously I'm tired and stressed out about everything. Fine, but that doesn't mean I get to take it out on this poor kid.

"He wants you to come," he whines, tears bright in his eyes, shaking like a leaf.

"I'm sorry," I say, suddenly overwhelmed with regret.

He wipes at his tears, still cowered, and nods, backing away from me.

"Where?" I ask, making no move to stop his retreat.

He gives me fast directions, then turns and bolts away. God I'm a jerk. I've never been that way before, not even to people I hate.

Looking at my ratty clothes I'm wearing, real clothes in my opinion, I know that Tynan won't be happy if I show up like this. I'm not going to go overboard but dressing appropriately isn't too much to ask.

Twenty minutes later I'm walking down the hall towards the tournament. Cheers erupt echoing around me. Great, a crowd. I'm not in the mood for this but I feel compelled to keep Tynan happy at least until I get what I want.

I know his fate and mine are intertwined. That alone keeps me jumping through his ridiculous hoops. I'm sure, in his mind, he sees these things as welcome distractions from the waiting.

I don't see it that way. I want to move, get in action, find my Dad and get on about doing... what?

How exactly do I go about saving the world?

And there we have the crux of the problem. I don't know and none of those who are apparently supposed to help me do either. So I sit here. Waiting, hoping, and looking for some grand sign from heaven on hey, Aviella, do this and then things will turn out all right.

While I wait, I fall into bed with Tynan, clear him of his mark as a Horseman, and most likely screw up my relationship with all of my other male friends, which at this point are all I have.

So maybe I do need more distractions.

Two bulky guards stand at the door I was given directions to and they nod as I walk up. One of them opens the door, bowing his head reverentially.

Seriously, he bowed his head? What the hell, Tynan? This is getting out of hand.

I walk out onto an observation deck. Tynan, Alaric, and Shen stand at the railing looking down. The moment I walk in, all three of them turn around.

"No way," Alaric hisses, his face contorting with anger.

"Tynan!" Shen exclaims.

I look at each of them in turn, confused myself.

"That's what changed," Alaric says. "You did it without us, without telling us even!"

"The time hasn't been correct," Tynan says, smooth and unflustered.

Under the façade, he's seething with barely suppressed anger.

"Not correct?" Shen asks.

"Boys," I say, intervening. "Whatever your discussion, I

came to see a tournament. Can you argue with each other later?"

The three of them stop glaring at each other and turn their full attention to me.

"Of course," Alaric says, composure falling over his face like a curtain dropping.

Shen nods too, then holds up a hand and one of their 'darlings' rushes forward with a tray of drinks followed by another who has a tray of canapes.

I take a drink and move to stand in the middle of the three dragons. I'm feeling bold and even a bit possessive of all three of them. Their gloomy, sour attitudes lift when I position myself so that I have Tynan on my left, Shen on my right, and Alaric is behind me.

When I look over the balcony, I see two large shirtless men engaged in battle below us. Various weapons are strewn about the dirt floor of the arena, but these two are apparently happy to beat each other senseless with their bare knuckles.

When one of them lands a solid blow on the other, blood flies out of his mouth, and something in me cheers at the sight. I cheer loudly as the one who was hit stumbles backwards, barely keeping himself upright.

I had expected to be bored, but something about this is primal and exciting. Two men, one versus another, with no certain outcome in sight.

Wait.

That's not me. I don't like violence like this. What am I thinking?

Once I realize this it becomes clear, again, that it's the effect of the connection I've established with Tynan. I'm feeling what he feels, but it's confusing, because at first it seems to be my thoughts, not his. This is going to be a problem.

Tearing my eyes away from the fight, I excuse myself

from the boys. Reluctantly they let me out, and I walk along the balcony trying to clear my head. Sort out what are my thoughts and feelings from his.

"You think you're so special," a female says, stepping in front of me and putting a hand on my chest, pushing me backwards.

"Excuse me?" I ask.

She has ice-blue eyes that bore into me. She's thin, gaunt, as are most of the 'darlings', but the force she pushes with takes me by surprise, and I stumble back. My blood boils and my heart pounds. Glaring at the girl, I straighten, crack my neck, then smile.

"You're going to regret that," I growl.

"Bring it, bitch," she snarls.

In a flash, she grabs my shirt and lifts me off my feet, carrying me towards the edge of the balcony. My vision turns red as magic surges. Static electricity crackles across my skin, then suddenly there's a crimson glow brightening the dimly lit area.

The girl stops, her eyes widening as she meets my gaze. I see her. Scared, simple, alone and desperate. Hunger rages inside me, a ravenous sensation that demands satiation.

Her mouth drops slack, drool runs out the corner, and the tiniest hints of magic pour out of her and into me, fulfilling the aching hunger.

Her grip loosens and I drop to my feet but I can't take my eyes from hers. I'm pulling her magic out of her, but it's more than that too. I'm feasting on her, her essence, everything that makes her *her*. She has to pay for what she did. I'll leave her a hollow shell, a husk to wander the halls of the bunker.

"Aviella, stop," Silas's voice cuts through the hunger, and he grabs my shoulder and turns me to him.

"Wha--"

I stop myself before I can finish the word. What was I

doing? The girl sobs. A glance over my shoulder, and she's on the ground bawling. Looking back at Silas, I see Shen and Alaric watching from behind him.

They had to have seen it, and yet they did nothing. This is one of their 'darlings', yet they do nothing? Their loyalty is a fickle and fleeting thing apparently.

Silas's face is a portrait of disappointment and regret. He opens his mouth, starts to speak, then snaps it shut. He gives a micro-shake of his head.

"Let's go," he says, taking my hand.

"No," I say, angry and petulant at the same time.

Who is he to order me around? His face hardens and his eyes have hard steel in them. His jaw tightens and I expect him to argue. I want him to argue with me.

"Okay," he says, taking the wind out of my sails.

He doesn't say anything else but moves to my side and stares down at the fight in progress in the arena.

Relishing the moment, no matter that he took all the triumph out of it, I lean against the railing and watch beside him. Out of the corner of my eye, Shen and Alaric have apparently lost interest now that I'm not about to kill someone. They're watching the fight, too. I don't see Tynan or have any idea where he's gotten to now.

The silence isn't comfortable, at all. Watching Silas out of the corner of my eye, I keep looking for something, anything I can latch on to. An anchor to be angry with him about, something I can use.

I'm not sure why I'm doing this, it feels right is all I can say. As the minutes tick by and there's nothing, I get more and more antsy with it. This need to show him. To one-up him somehow.

"I slept with Tynan," I say, impulsively.

Part of me is shocked at my own words, but another part of me is elated when I see the crack in his facade. His eyes widen as they dart to me and his magic scans over me seeking the truth of my words.

A smile plays along my lips that I can't suppress. I've got him, there Methuselah, there are still some things that can surprise you, and I'm one of them.

"I see," he says, carefully schooling his face, voice neutral. "Please come with me, now."

He said please which seems to cut through the strange need I have to make him feel wrong, so I take his hand and let him lead us away from the tournament.

He leads the way quickly through the tunnels and to my own rooms. Our journey is done in silence, but now I don't mind because I've won. I don't know what it is I think I've won, but I'm damn proud of myself for having done it.

I open the door and step aside, letting him in first. As he passes me, the scent of him fills my nose, and I'm suddenly consumed by desire. I want him. No, I need him, now.

"Aviella," he says as I close the door and lock it.

"Silas," I say his name in a low, long breath, staring at him with half-lidded eyes.

I move across the room to him, swaying my hips, caressing him with my magic as I close. Desire plays across his face, and he can't hide the bulge rising in his pants.

Before I close with him, he takes my shoulders and then lifts my chin up with one hand. He stares into my eyes, getting close in a completely not sexy way.

"Your eyes," he says, shaking his head.

"You like them?" I ask.

"They're red," he says.

"Late night," I answer.

"I think it's more than that," he says, dropping his hand from my chin.

I put a hand on his chest and slowly move it up to his neck. He stiffens, but encouragingly he doesn't move away.

When I touch the skin of his neck, a shock runs up my arm, tingling, as the raw contact somehow causes our magic to interact.

He grabs my head, wrapping a hand in my hair and jerks me forward, his lips smashing against mine. His free hand drops to my ass, squeezing, and I thrust my hips against him, grinding on the hard bulge.

It's nice, so sweet and nice and everything I want, but then something rises forward. He's in control.

No, I can't let that be.

Driving my tongue past his tight lips I invade his mouth while pushing my hand down between us and stroking his cock through his pants. He groans into my mouth and that need to control is satisfied.

He's mine. I'm going to take him.

Silas pulls back, hands on my shoulders.

"No," he says.

Smiling, I knock his arms aside with one hand while taking a grip on his cock. His eyes close, and he groans with pleasure. Now he lowers his lips to mine, his tongue finding and dancing with mine.

We work our way to a chair, clothes falling as we move. Reaching the chair, I turn and press my ass against his cock. He puts his hands on my hips then moves one hand to my neck, pushing me down.

I bend over and grab the arms of the chair, then open my legs to welcome him.

He accepts the invitation, his cock sliding into me until he's fully seated. I gasp my pleasure as it fills me.

He twines one hand in my hair and the other rests on my ass. He pulls out slowly until only the tip is in, then he thrusts forward hard, the force causing my head to press into the soft cushioning of the chair.

Pushing back against him as he thrusts in and pulling off, we develop a rhythm.

Our magic slams together with each push in and retreats. Mixing, melding, then separating once more. Each time we come together, our magical essence joins too, and when we pull apart, parts of the other comes along.

My awareness shifts, creating a strange, doubling sensation. My body, the pleasure of joining with him, the fulfilling of desire, but layered over that, and in some way I don't understand, more potent, is the joining of our magical energies.

The intensity of our desire melds the energy, creating something new.

Silas slows, the immediacy of need resolving as we join. His hands trace up and down my sides, reaching around to grab my breasts and tease the nipples.

Every sensation is doubled, occurring both in my body and in my magic at the same time. I'm carried away with sheer bliss.

We shift positions, then after a time, we move to the bed. As he climbs on top of me and I welcome him in, staring into his eyes, we join. It's sudden, a sensation as if breaking through a thin protective wall.

Instantly I'm aware of him with a new depth. The weight of his years crashes in, and in a moment I'm lost in them. Ages of man flashing through my thoughts, memories, his memories. Nomadic tribes through to the Ancient Egyptians, and marching forward through time. Seeing wars and wonders alike, living lifetime after lifetime, pursuing knowledge and understanding throughout them all.

His lips caress mine, his body pressing on top, and the flood of memories continues.

His magic is different than mine, less volatile, but also not the same in how it flows. It can be used in defense and offense but it's more suited to finding hidden secrets. Learning, getting insights, and finding new understandings.

As the differences dawn on me, suddenly, my own magic surges. My body feels like a breaker switch hit with too much electricity. I'm riding lightning made of pure magic. Crackling sounds accent the moans and groans of our lovemaking.

As my body stiffens, back arches, toes curl, an orgasm with an intensity I've never experienced rips through my body and my magic.

Embracing him, with arms and magic, I pull him tight, and we hold each other, panting, until the overwhelm of sensations passes.

He collapses on top of me, breathing heavily, his heart pounding against my chest so hard I feel and hear it. Rising up, he places soft kisses on my lips, across my face, then he pulls out and lies down beside me.

The connection we share is wide-open and strong. I know what he's thinking, how he's feeling. Sense his satisfaction tinged with regret and concern over what this will mean.

I don't feel any regret. The anger is gone as well, that burning need to dominate and be in control. Now that I'm no longer under its influence I see clearly that is Tynan's nature invading my own.

"I should go," Silas says.

Shifting to my side to see him better, I arch an eyebrow.

"You sure?" I ask, probing along the connection looking for why he feels the need to go.

There, I've got it. He doesn't want to cause problems. A slow smile spreads across my face as he frowns, staring.

"Interesting," he says, then shakes his head and climbs off the bed.

He gathers his clothes, and I lasciviously enjoy the view. Once he's dressed he comes back into the bedroom where

I'm lounging, enjoying a sense of satisfaction that's been sorely missing.

"It's good, right?" I ask, genuinely curious.

"You are the very embodiment of good," he says without a trace of sarcasm in his voice or thoughts.

"I don't know about that," I say, sighing. "But it felt right, though."

"Yes," he says, a smile forming on his face.

My skin tingles, magic racing across it creating goosepimples in its passing. Silas walks over, kisses me gently, then leaves.

I'm aware of his thoughts as he walks down the halls. He's running through a list of books he hasn't finished translating, and one he hopes will be useful in understanding the symbols I drew.

Rolling onto my side, I pull the blankets over myself and smile as I drift off to sleep.

CHAPTER TEN

AVIELLA

*T*wo days pass without anything happening. Frustration is a constant companion.

Nothing is holding my attention, and in a most unusual twist, no one has come to visit. No Tynan, Efram, Silas or anyone. Alone, two days, with nothing to do.

I've been playing around with the new connection I have though, which has served to pass some of the time. Tynan, I can sense but not much else. An awareness of his mood and a knowing of what direction he is from me is all I get off the dragon.

Silas, well he started out more interesting, then I think he figured out what I was doing. At first I was able to connect to him fully. I could see what he was seeing, know his thoughts. I was actually enjoying this, and reading the book he was reading, which was super cool because I could understand it even though it was in a language I don't know. He knew it so I knew what he knew.

Then suddenly he closed his eyes and the connection was blocked. I can barely get a sense of direction to him from me now.

So that's a thing. Crappy thing, but a thing.

Now I'm bored. Where's Efram? It's weird for him to leave me alone for so long.

Left to my own devices, I've done everything I can think of to fill the time, including lots of introspection. That's probably not a bad thing. I'm still worried about hurting Efram.

I don't feel bad for what I've done. Maybe I should? I don't know, what's the morality for the Apocalypse after all?

It doesn't matter, because what I've done was right. I know it, when I joined with Tynan and then Silas the connection to each of them has grown stronger. It's almost as if we're bonded now.

Yeah, that's a good term for it. Bonded. The act of joining our bodies tied the bindings of our magic together stronger, tighter, or something like that.

Silas probably knows, and if the jerk wasn't blocking me, I could find a word or concept for it I'm sure, but he is. Rolling my eyes, I sigh and put down the book in my hand.

I miss television.

At least with a television you could vegetate out and somehow the magical moving pictures kept your thoughts from spinning in circles.

Thinking about that, it's not good is it? Television had a hypnotic effect really, and that is, I'm sure, one of the things that led to the downfall of the world. A strange certainty fills me that it was part of the shadow conspiracy plan. The great evil I'm fated to fight.

If I ever get out of this bunker. If I ever find my Dad. If, if, if, too damn many if's!

Bouncing to my feet, I glare around the empty room as if daring it to either fight me or entertain me. It, of course, does nothing. Thanks room, no help at all.

Fine, I'll take a walk. If Efram isn't coming to me, I'll go to him. He doesn't know about Silas and Tynan, does he?

If he does, I need to find him even more. I can't believe he'd be sulking but if he is, then I need to see him and handle it. Closing my eyes I try something. Reaching out with my magic, I imagine it as pulsing waves that move out in a circle from me passing through the entire bunker. In my mind's eye it's like a sonar screen.

I'm concentrating on Efram and my desire to find him. He's the one I want. Where is he?

It works, or at least it seems to because the feeling that he's below me comes in loud and clear. It makes sense, I know he's been hanging out with the witches in the under-bunker area. If nothing else that's a good place to go look for him.

Decision made I head out into the halls of the bunkers. The residents of the bunker shoot me envious looks causing a mix of delight and regret. Now I know the delight is an aspect of Tynan's nature.

Fortunately I also know that it's not actually delight but something more primal. He's a dragon, and by his nature, he expects everyone and everything to submit to him. It's the submission to his dominating power and personality. I don't think he experiences it the same way I do.

It's not pleasure, for him it's the way it should be. It's not my nature though, so it interprets differently. I, the real me, feels nothing but regret for them.

The sadness I feel when I look at them is almost overwhelming. They're doing the best they can but they've lost hope. The game they play is the one thing they cling to in an effort to exert some control over their own lives.

It's so fundamentally human, to try and overcome no matter the odds against you. A testament to the human spirit contrasted by the most awful of circumstances.

When I get to the undertunnels, the looks change from jealousy to suspicion. They know my connection to the dragon overlords, and they, more or less, hate me for it.

Ignoring their looks, I march through until a large burly man with a wisp of a girl next to him steps into my path, blocking me.

"You're not welcome," he growls.

"Right," I say, looking around him. "I'm here to see Efram."

"He's busy," the girl throws in.

"I'm sure he is, but he'll want to see me."

"No," big and burly says, crossing his arms over and puffing out his chest.

"Impressive," I snark, my eyes burn as magic rises and there is the soft buzz of static electricity. "Want to test me and see what I can do?"

My voice drops lower, to almost a growl. Fear plays behind his eyes, but he keeps his face stoic. The girl takes a step back as the tension rises.

"What is this?" Merrick asks, walking up behind the two.

"She shouldn't be here," the burly guy says.

"Says who?" Merrick asks.

Burly guy drops his arms and turns to Merrick.

"She's with them," he says and there's almost a whining to his voice now.

"Right," Merrick says, meeting the man's glare. "And?"

Burly guy shakes his head then turns and walks away, the girl staying at his side as they leave.

"Nice welcoming committee," I say. "Might be different next time."

The last I yell past Merrick and take great satisfaction in seeing the burly man's back stiffen. The girl puts a hand on his arm stopping him from turning around with a soft-spoken word.

"That's not necessary," Merrick says, shaking his head.

"Neither is big and burly trying to threaten me," I retort.

"Right," Merrick says turning and leading the way to an area that apparently serves as his office. "Why are you here?"

"I'm looking for Efram, mostly," I say, taking a seat across from the rickety-looking desk.

"He'll be here shortly," Merrick answers. "But I was wanting to talk to you anyway. I think we found your father."

"What?" I'm on my feet in an instant. "Where? When do we leave?"

"Calm down," Merrick says, holding his hands up and making calming motions.

"Calm down?" I ask, my voice cracking. "I have to save him."

"I know," he says. "You will. We'll help, but first things first."

"What's happening?" Efram asks, entering the fray.

When I turn to face him, his eyes widen and he takes a step back the moment he sees me. His reaction gives me pause, as it's not what I would expect.

"Efram?" I ask, stepping towards him in confusion.

His face is a blank mask and he doesn't retreat again. He does force a smile.

"Aviella, what's happened?" he asks.

"Merrick says they found my father," I say, the words pouring out in a rush.

"We've found a clue," Merrick corrects from behind me.

"A clue then, whatever, it's more than we've had yet. We have to go, I know he's in trouble. I have to save him."

"Okay, good," Efram says.

He's still looking at me oddly.

"What?" I snap.

He shakes his head, frowns, then moves past me and takes a seat.

"He's probably wondering why your eyes are red," Merrick says.

"Red? I haven't been sleeping," I say, turning to the two men who are both staring at me like I've grown a second head.

"I said red, not bloodshot," Merrick says.

"Oh," I say, holding my hand up in front of my eyes and noticing for the first time that there's a soft, red glow emanating from them.

Damn it. It's Tynan bleeding into me again. That's the source of the anger and the way I acted with that burly guy earlier. I've got to get this under control.

"What happened, Aviella?" Efram asks.

"Nothing, really... I'm..." I can't say what I need to say to him here, not in front of Merrick. "My magic seems to be developing again."

It's a lame finish but not a complete lie. Merrick, for his part, accepts it at face value, but the look on Efram's face makes it clear he has questions, but he's smart enough to file them for later.

"What do we know?" Efram asks Merrick, changing the subject, for his sake or mine I'm not sure though.

"Rumors only but someone fitting his description was spotted in a mega-church bunker," Merrick answers.

"Some of those are still standing?" Efram asks.

"Yes," Merrick says. "Unfortunately."

Mega-church bunkers. Home to the most fanatical, crazy, bonkers, absolutely insane zealots to survive the Apocalypse. They're all convinced that they were either somehow missed by the Rapture, or that they were intentionally left behind to fulfill God's Will on Earth.

Only problem with that is 'God's Will' is what they're told it is by their leaders who are all even more insane than the run-of-the-mill penitents. That's not good news.

Of course any news is better than no news, which is what I've had besides my own feelings, and certainty he was alive out there somewhere.

"Fine, which one, and how soon can we leave?" I ask.

"It's not that easy," Merrick says.

"Why not?" I counter.

"It's dangerous for one," he says. "Two, I have to care for my people too. I can't leave them defenseless against the dragons."

"You and the dragons," I exclaim exasperation heavy in my voice. "You know they're not that bad, right? There's more to them than meets the eye."

"You would certainly think that," he says, his eyes cold steel.

"And what do you mean by that?" I snap, Tynan's angry nature filtering into me once again.

This time I see it happening so I pull on Silas and his stoic nature to bolster my own natural tendencies and resist the dragon's impulsive aspects.

"I mean what I said," he says, firm but not overly challenging.

"Okay," I say, sighing. Efram watches me closely but says nothing. "I get it. I'm telling you though, they're not all bad. At least they don't want to be."

"Well that makes everything oh, so much better," he says. "If they do all their evil, but they don't really want to, that makes it all good."

"You're being a sarcastic ass," I snap.

"And you're being a foolish idealist," he says.

We glare at each other, but now the anger is my own. I'm tired of his attitude, and he's putting another block between finding my father and me.

Magic crackles in the air, responding to my anger and mood.

"We can't lose our heads," Efram says. "We're too close, and you two need to get it under control."

"Right," I say, dropping back into the chair, and exhaling a breath I didn't realize I'd been holding. The wisdom of his words cuts through my anger, and I'm left empty.

"I'm not going to argue the point with you," Merrick says before he sits back himself. "The only thing that matters is actions. If they start acting like they give a damn, and stop the Hunger Games action happening above us, then I might be inclined to believe you. Until then, Dragons are the enemy."

We stare at each other for a long moment while I turn over his words. How many times have I said this to Tynan? Looking at it that way, Merrick is right.

"Good enough," I agree, and in a gesture of friendship, I offer my hand.

He takes it and we shake firmly.

"I'm willing to be wrong," he says softly. "For the fate of all humanity, I hope I am."

"I think you are," I say. "But only time will tell."

"Right," he says.

"And with that, I think we should take our leave," Efram says.

"What about my dad?" I ask, looking between the two men.

As much as I try to ignore it, there's an empty ache inside of me that only he can fill. At times it's what drives me more than anything.

"I'll follow up on what we know," Merrick answers.

It's the best I'm going to get and I know it. Nodding agreement, I follow Efram out and we leave the undertunnels, making our way back up towards my suite of rooms.

Once again I'm walking in silence with one of my men, my sweet protectors. Efram is the first of the men I've collected on my journey, and probably the sweetest of the bunch. He's also the one I most don't want to hurt.

Which means I need to talk to him about Tynan. Silas I'm not worried about, immediately anyway. Tynan though, he's a braggart, and I have no doubt he'll let it slip, intentionally or not.

I unlock my door and walk in, expecting him to follow, but when I glance back, he's still standing in the doorway.

"Coming in?" I ask.

"I've some things to tend to," he says, not meeting my eyes.

"Oh," I say, the gulf between us widening.

Reaching out with magic, I feel for him, but he has shields up blocking me. Instantly I know I could push past them. They're not strong enough to keep me out if I really want in. That's new, but no way I'm doing that. He's my friend.

"Efram, come in, for a little bit at least, please," I add the please on at the end when he still seems to be hesitant.

He looks grim, but nods and walks in, shutting the door behind him. I offer a drink but he declines, though he does sit in one of my overstuffed chairs.

He sits stiffly, hands on his knees and eyes looking around the room, but never lingering on me for long. Okay, well this is awkward.

I make myself a cup of tea before sitting down across from him, pulling my legs up under myself and blowing on the hot liquid. I'm hoping he'll speak first, if I wait long enough.

When I'm half-way through the cup of tea, he clears his throat then looks directly at me.

"When?" he asks.

"Huh?" I look up at him both in surprise and non-comprehension.

"When did it happen?" he asks, swallowing hard.

Furrowing my brow, I look over his question and try to figure out what he means. Suddenly it dawns on me.

"Oh," I say, setting the tea down on a small table. He waits, silent, while I gather my thoughts.

"Couple of days ago," I say. "It's what I wanted to talk to you about."

"Okay," he says, but the hurt is so obvious on his face and in his voice there's an answering ache in my chest.

"Efram," I say. "It changes nothing."

"Of course," he says. "It's fine. It won't change anything."

"How did you know?" I ask. "I wanted to tell you myself is all."

"Your eyes," he says. "The red glow and I can feel his magic mixing in to yours."

"Oh," I say, nodding. "Are you okay?"

"Of course I am," he smiles. "You don't owe me an explanation. There is no commitment between any of us."

The hurt is gone from his voice and fading from his face. His smile seems genuine, but more than that, it's beautiful. He's beautiful, in a manly, rugged way of course. Instinctively I'm reaching out with my magic, caressing his shields lightly, seeking permission to come in as I always have.

Rising to my feet I cross the room and lean over him, arms on the chair, my face an inch from his.

"Efram," I say, locking onto his eyes. "Please."

Subtly he stiffens and I don't miss it.

"Aviella," he says.

"You know," I tell him. "You know how I feel about you."

His eyes give it away, all his pent-up feelings for me, the desire and, dare I say it? Yes, the love. He loves me, and in some way, I love him too.

"And I you," he says, so softly I strain to hear it.

Moving closer, our lips are centimeters apart. His breath

has a hint of cinnamon to it, I feel his heart beating, his magic wraps around me like I want his arms to.

"Kiss me," I order.

Our lips graze, the barest of touches, not nearly enough to fulfill my need. He grabs my arms and pushes me back.

"Not like this," he says, rising to his feet and forcing me back as he does so with my arms pinned in his vise-like grip. "I would never take advantage of you when you're in a state of confusion."

"When am I not in a state of confusion?" I ask, petulant.

"It will happen," he smiles, his eyes heavy and a tiredness coming off of him in waves. "Soon, I hope."

He turns and walks out my door without looking back.

Great. That went absolutely great, not.

Sighing I flop down in the chair, sip my now-cold tea, and then out of sheer lack of anything else to do, pick up the book I've been trying to read, and open it to the marked page.

CHAPTER ELEVEN

AVIELLA

I'm tired. So damn tired. Sleep hasn't only been elusive, it's more something I dread.

Nightmares plague me constantly. They never let up, and now, with possible news of my dad, they're worse than ever. I woke up early, really early, in a cold sweat, gripping the sheets tight and panting. The room was electric as magic crackled around me without a target to incinerate.

And now it's another day. Another day of... nothing. Another day of waiting.

How long can I stand this? Where are Rafe and Nathaniel? I really think they should have been back by now, but no one else seems to agree. It's always, they'll be fine, Aviella. They'll be back soon.

The sixth trumpet has sounded, the four chained angels have raised their armies and march across the world, leaving death and destruction in their wake. How do we know that Rafe and Nathaniel are safe?

How is anyone safe when even Shen and Alaric's bunker fell to the trumpet army.

All things considered, is it any wonder I'm not sleeping? I

keep seeing that symbol when I sleep. Sometimes I see my dad being tortured, sometimes it's Rafe or Nathaniel, but always there's the symbol and the whispering voice telling me I can stop it all.

Right, me. Orphan Aviella, so special, fated to save the world. What a bunch of bullshit.

I don't want to save the world—I want to save my dad. How am I supposed to save all of humanity if I can't save one man?

After pushing the fruit and eggs around on my plate, I give up on eating, and drop the fork. I pour more coffee, lean back, and sip while sending out my magical awareness. I'm not sure what I'm looking for, nothing particular really, but there's always the dim hope that I'll find Rafe, Nathaniel, or dimmest of all, my father.

The sensations of doing this are strange. An awareness of the life forces that my magic encompasses is part of it, but I've figured out I have to focus on a target. The magic has to be guided. It needs a purpose.

This is probably the biggest thing Silas has taught me about magic. It is, at the end, a channel to make your intention happen in the universe.

That's why my magic was so wild before my mentors taught me to control it. My intentions were as wild as it was. My magic manifested when I was young, alone, and an outcast. Picked on, uncertain of myself, my desires were to be left alone. Looking back, only the hand of divine providence can explain how I never seriously hurt someone. I did tear up a lot of property in the orphanage where I was raised, but never more than some cuts and bruises to those who picked on me.

Even when I extend myself to the limit, nothing stands out. Sighing, I open my eyes, down the last of the coffee, and stand up to stretch.

My days are filled with nothing. Tynan and the dragons keep throwing events to distract me, and while they annoy me, I hate to admit they're almost welcome. Sitting here, in my room, alone, knowing I should be doing... something, anything, is in its own way worse.

"This sucks," I say out loud to no one because as usual, I'm alone.

Young, orphanage me, would be so happy. Now, I'm not used to it. I've traveled with my companions for so long, to have them separated from me leaves an empty ache behind.

My throat is thick, closing on itself as the sensations come forward once more. I'm alone. Tears swell in the corners of my eyes.

"Come on, Aviella," I say out loud, hoping the sound of my own voice will counteract the oppressive silence of the room.

Hugging myself tight, I lean back in the chair, pull my feet up, and close my eyes. Maybe a nap will pass some time. Anything to escape the way this is making me feel.

My emotions vacillate wildly since my merging with Tynan. Silas helped, but somehow he's able to control how much of him I access. It's a storm inside and I, the me that is me, feels a lot like I'm a small boat in a typhoon. Tossed around by waves that are a hundred feet high and thrown from one feeling to the next.

I have to be careful because I'm not sure what's me and what's one of them. It's making my emotional state volatile and I'm likely to explode at any time.

Focusing on nothing I try to calm my thoughts and mind as Silas taught me. The noise, doubts, and worries are outside me. I'm center, here, and it's quiet. There is only me.

Something calls to me, and instinctively I reach for it.

It's all over.

That wasn't my thought. Concentrating, I try to spot the source.

No one cares about me. There's no point.

A depth of despair crashes over me, and I'm drowning in it. Opening my eyes, gasping, I struggle to breathe even though it's all happening in my mind only. My magic makes it real, it *is* real, but not my despair.

"No!" I scream, suddenly I see a young, beautiful girl standing next to a railing.

I know that view, it's where they held the tournament. That's at least three maybe four stories up. She's going to jump!

I'm running out my door I'm halfway down the hall before I realize I'm barefoot, but there's no time to turn back. Her pain pounds in my chest, her thoughts echo in my head.

Flowing out to her with magic, I try to reach her, give her reassurance, but I can't get past the black cloud that surrounds her.

She's too thin, too lost, she's given up.

"Look out!" I scream, pushing past a crowd standing in one of the junctures.

They turn in confusion as I slam into them, fighting my way through their haphazard attempts to get out of my way.

"Move, damn it, move!"

There are so many of them pressing in on me that I can't get through. I have to reach her! My vision covers over with red, my sight narrowing down to my singular goal. Magic explodes out of me in a force wave and the crowd is thrown into the walls, clearing the path.

I don't look back.

She jumps. I feel it, feel the air rushing past her, hear the screams of onlookers.

She's falling.

"NO!" I scream, my own voice tearing my throat with its force.

I take a left and run down a hall that should lead out into the arena. Two burly men are running too but I catch them.

"You can't—" one of them says.

"Move!" I order, my voice guttural and commanding.

They step aside with a jerk, coming to immediate attention. Ignoring them I run through the door that's just ahead.

Looking around wildly, I'm in the arena, she's not here.

Where is she?

"Ahhhh!" someone screams, and I look up towards the source of the sound.

There, she's still falling. Magic surges and I cup my hands, calling it to me, shaping it and then throw them up forcing the air itself to my will slowing her descent.

I only hope it's enough.

My rage burns, boiling my blood. Stupid fool of a girl, throwing her life away. Nothing is worth it. Nothing.

She lands with a soft thud on the packed dirt and I storm over. There are cuts on her arms, and a wound in her chest.

She didn't jump, she was stabbed, then pushed. Her eyelids flutter, her lips tremble, and trickle of blood runs from her nose as more soaks her left side.

Kneeling beside her, I cup her cheek and put a hand on her chest, close to the wound. Closing my eyes, I flow into her, willing her body to heal.

Warmth floods through me and the red of my vision is burned away by whiteness. Her erratic heartbeat stabilizes under my hand, and then I hear her gasp loudly.

When I open my eyes, she is looking up at me in confusion. She shakes her head.

"You're beautiful," she whispers, her eyes wide.

"What happened here?" Tynan's voice cuts through the moment.

"Is she okay?" Silas asks as he skids to a stop next to us.

I inhale deeply and everything inside of me shifts and

finally, I'm me. I don't know if it is having the two men in front of me at the same time, or maybe it took time to sort itself out. The mix of them into me feels, somehow, like it's complete. I'm me again.

Try explaining that to someone. My life is so weird. Oh yeah, I slept with this guy and his personality invaded mine and almost took control. Well it did, sometimes, and you know that was fun, not.

I open my eyes and smile at the girl.

"You saved me," she says, grabbing and pulling me into a hug that makes it almost impossible to breathe.

Looking up at the two men, I try to give them a 'help me' look. Silas looks, like he always does, interested, like he's studying. Tynan has a look of amusement and a wry smile.

"Okay," I say, working to extricate myself from the girl.

As I push her back, a hint of power in her reaches out and my magic touches it. Suddenly it blossoms then explodes. She glows blindingly white and levitates three inches off the floor as magical light pours out of her.

I fall back onto my ass, shielding my eyes from the bright light. It connects to my magic and pulls, sucking my energy into her.

"Uh, help?" she asks, her voice quavering.

Blinking to adjust my eyes, I see her look from Silas, to Tynan, to me, uncertain what is happening. Her magic sucks on mine like a babe learning to nurse, pulling and drawing it into her. I try to stop the flow, but its demand increases, taking more.

"An innocent," Tynan says.

He exhales the word, and there's a look on his face that I can't read. The connection between us is suddenly closed, he slams it shut, pursing his lips, jaw tightening. He's not angry, that I'd recognize, this is something else entirely.

I don't have time to deal with his problem, because he's

right. This girl is one of the innocents. Magic-bearing people who, by whatever divine gift, are free of sin. They're special and are somehow tied into my grand fate of saving the world. More than that, she's draining my magic at an alarming rate, using it to power her own rebirthing.

The light fades and she settles back to the ground, shaking in the aftermath. I'm drained, empty of my own magical energy and barely able to keep myself upright.

"You're okay," I reassure her, placing an arm around her shoulders as much to hold myself upright as to give her reassurance.

She shivers a bit more, then gets a grip on herself, and moves to rise to her feet.

"What happened?" Silas asks.

"I... I was..." she looks up above us to the point she fell from. "I'd lost a beauty contest, I was so depressed. I went up there to be alone and..."

"Go on" Tynan says.

My vision is wavering, it's an effort of will to focus my attention. I've never felt so empty in my life.

"Then someone came out of the shadows, and they swung a knife at me!" her voice cracks and she looks at her side, hands going to the blood staining her shirt. "How?"

"Aviella is a healer of some skill," Tynan says.

His eyes glow crimson as he looks at me. That strange look is still on his face, but he's closed the connection, and I can't reach in to find out what he's feeling.

"Thank you!" she exclaims, grabbing and squeezing me again.

Okay, we have a hugger here. I'm too tired to resist as she squeezes me half to death. She lets me go after a long, awkward moment passes and stares at her side.

"Was that... light… was that you?" she asks.

"That was all you," I say, giving her the best smile I can muster.

"What?" she exclaims.

"Aviella, there are better ways to handle this," Silas admonishes.

"You've got power you are only now manifesting," I explain, ignoring Silas and his dirty looks. "You've got a lot to look forward to."

"Power? Me? Really?" she asks, holding her hand up in front of her face and turning them back and forth. "Cool!"

I nod and cross my arms over my chest giving Silas an 'I told you so' look. The slightest of frowns is his only reaction.

Looking at the girl, there's a lot of turmoil in her and a bit of darkness. She'll need to be trained and cared for, but she'll be all right.

"A lot's going to happen," I say to her then look over at Silas. "Can you contact the mages?"

"They'll be on their way," he says.

"Good," I say.

"The mages?" the girl asks.

"Yeah," I say, forcing a smile. "Friends of ours. They take care of people like you."

"Oh," she says.

Fear and uncertainty play across her face which I can read as clearly as if I'm reading a book. I remember that feeling well, and it evokes a deep empathy.

"It's going to be okay," I say. "I know you don't know me, but please believe me. Your life is about to change, and from what I can tell it's going to be for the better."

She grimaces, braces herself, then nods and smiles.

"Right," she says. "Face forward and all."

"Exactly," I agree.

"Silas, can you take care of her until they arrive?" I say it like I'm asking, but it's also an order.

The look he gives me makes it clear he catches the intent. At first I expect him to balk, but he nods and takes the girls arm.

"Come with me," he says glancing quickly between Tynan and me.

He leads her away, leaving Tynan and me alone. I'm barely able to keep my eyes open, but I have to deal with him. I have to know.

"All right," I say, wavering on my feet, "spill it."

"Spill it?" he asks, a wry look on his face.

"You know exactly what I mean," I reply.

Slowly he nods that he does, but he doesn't speak. His eyes look into the distance seeing something far away, and an air of deep melancholy falls over both of us. Patiently I wait, giving him time to figure out what to say.

"She was innocent," he says focusing his eyes back on me when at last he speaks. "Truly innocent."

"Yes," I say, not understanding the implications that he's obviously meaning.

A wan smile drifts across his face, and he shakes his head.

"I wonder, how many such have my brethren and I destroyed," he says.

There's emptiness in those words. It's not an uncaring, blank emptiness, it's a hollow abyss that threatens to swallow all with its consuming hunger.

"Oh," I say, unable to form more words.

"More," he continues. "Her innocent soul doesn't compare to yours. You are purer than any soul I've ever encountered, and I wonder how I've not seen it before."

The humbleness in his words is shocking. Tynan, always confident and full of himself, abasing himself to me in such a way leaves me without a response.

There's more to his words. More that comes through the connection that we have together because though he's trying to keep it closed, he can't hold back the emotions that are flowing.

I'm aware of his trying to hide it, but he can't. The feelings are too strong, too much to be held in check. They swirl around, lifting me up and tearing me at the same time. We're standing on a precipice. Do we jump, or do we ignore?

I don't know, but it's clear what the dragon's feelings are for me. All I can think about is the other men in my life and how this might affect them. I can't live without all of them and I know, with certainty, I can't fulfill my fate without them.

Choppy waters and I have to navigate them carefully.

Suddenly my body is too heavy. I can't possibly hold it up any longer. My eyes drift closed. I will them to stay open, but they don't care. Dimly I'm aware of the ground racing up, then I'm floating.

CHAPTER TWELVE

I'm on a dark cloud moving through space and time. Outside of my bubble is an awareness of the world, but it's distant, not part of me really.

I've never felt more exhausted. Depleted. I've got nothing left. When the girl tapped into my magic, she pulled out everything I had and then some. All I want is to sleep and let the black emptiness encompass me.

Some part of me is aware of Tynan carrying me and that we're entering my rooms, but it's something that barely matters. The tiredness is too much. I've got nothing left to give.

Something whispers, calling to me, telling me to let it all go. Set down my burdens and let someone else pick them up. I've done my part. I've done enough.

The appeal of that is almost more than I can resist. I'd love to give it all over. Someone else can be the one fated to save the world. Anyone but me. The voice grows louder as I listen and the appeal of it grows.

"Aviella," Tynan's voice cuts through the shadows and the exhaustion. "Stay with me."

Something about his words, a sensation, a meaning more than is apparent. They call to me. I shouldn't give over to the whispers from the darkness. I shouldn't, but they're so loud, so inviting. If I listen, all the pain will go away. All the stress, the worries will be done.

I have to force myself to look, to make my eyes flutter open. Tynan's smiling face is inches from mine. He's so hand-some, an incredibly sexy man with strong cheekbones and sharp, brilliant eyes.

His lips close with mine, anchoring me into the moment. Pulling me from the shadows.

It's a pull, and suddenly it's a fight. The shadows cling to me, gripping and cloying, unwilling to let me go. Mentally I scream, fear rising as I realize I can't leave them behind. They've a hold on me and aren't going to give up.

"Tynan," I gasp into our kiss as his hands roam across my body.

I can barely feel him touching me. The sensation is filtered, distant, almost like I'm watching it but not feeling it. A scene in a movie I'm watching or a memory of being touched.

"Aviella," he breathes, kissing my cheek, down my neck, pulling my shirt loose.

New energies approach even as his magic caresses over me, calling me back. The cloying shadows' hold on me is strong, but his energy keeps them from encroaching further. Then his brothers are there, standing on either side of my bed, watching as he kisses his way across my neck and between my breasts.

Groaning, I arch my back in response. Pleasure eases the shadows' grip.

Alaric and Shen's eyes are alight with delight, burning with passion and pleasure as they not only watch Tynan kissing his way along my body but they feel it with their magic adding theirs to his. The three of them call me back to them.

Slowly the newcomers undress, dropping their clothes to the ground. The sight of their sculpted bodies fans my stoked flames of desire into a raging inferno that burns in my core. The shadows incinerate before its burning intensity. No shadow can stand against the onslaught of my light.

Alaric and Shen climb onto the bed, their erect members jutting out before them, begging for my attention. Their magic caresses my skin, and even though they have yet to touch me, I feel them.

Tynan kisses his way down my stomach, his intention clear, and his brothers close as well. I grab their members, one in each hand, and stroke softly as Tynan lowers himself into my intimacy.

His tongue is a scholar of pleasure. As he works my delicate folds, the sensations drive me wild. Gripping the two dicks tightly, I buck wildly in response to his attentions.

Shen and Alaric's hands touch where they can reach, and their magic caresses the rest of my skin.

Sensation on overload, no thoughts form, only an intensity of pleasure. It's too much for my brain, overwhelming and complete.

Tynan is aggressive with his tongue, driving deep, exploring every fold, leaving no part of me untouched. Alaric leans in, kissing me passionately as he plunges his tongue into my mouth.

Shen's hands are on my breasts, kneading them, then moving to toy with my hard nipples.

No part of me is untouched. Their attention flows across me as a gentle river, nothing going unnoticed or unattended.

Alaric breaks our kiss, rising and moving forward, presenting his member to my mouth, and I take it greedily. He rocks back and forth, pushing in and out, groaning.

I moan around the fullness in my mouth. Alaric grabs my head and forces himself deep until he's entering my throat.

Tynan drives his tongue deep inside my pussy, while Shen grips my breasts tight, and I do the same to his cock.

All four of us moan loudly, our voices joining in unison, creating a chorus of pleasure.

Sensations in my body build, but it's so much more than that alone. Each thrust into me, my mouth and my pussy both, drive magical energy into me. The points of contact are direct sources. Hungrily, I take in their magic as I take in their bodies. Welcoming, needing, letting it and them fill me.

Alaric pulls out of my mouth, groaning his pleasure, and I gasp in air as Shen pulls my head around to his cock.

Gently, he pushes past my lips and fucks my mouth. Blindly reaching, I find Alaric's dick and stroke its length, still wet with the spit of my mouth.

Tynan moves his attention to my clit, winding up my pleasure until I'm so tight I have to give in. There is no holding back the pleasure any longer.

It bursts through my body with a rush, and as it does, my magic furthers its own recharging.

As my first orgasm passes, Tynan raises his head, kissing over my mound and up to my stomach. He rises onto his knees and positions his cock at my opening.

There's no hesitation as he drives himself in to his hilt, while at the same time Shen grabs my head and shoves me forward so that Alaric's dick is forced into my throat.

Magic explodes through my body, a battery drinking in all that they can give, hungry and wanting more.

There's not enough, I need more, I'm only starting to feel life return to me.

Tynan sets a pace of driving in and out that Alaric and Shen match. Shen pushing my head back and forth, Alaric driving with his hips. I grip Shen's cock tight, so no one is being left out.

It's heaven.

An instant's thought, I never imagined I'd be this girl, but that flies away. The girl who I was never knew there could be pleasure such as this.

Their attention flows over me as their bodies do. They're giving me all that they have. Their magic pouring into me, their bodies giving me pleasure. Their attention is all for me: I am the center and all that they desire.

At some unspoken signal, Tynan and Alaric pull out at the same time. The three men climb off the bed, and I'm left momentarily lost and wanting.

Tynan doesn't keep me waiting, he grabs me up, lifting me easily, and turning with me in his arms. He kisses me, soft but insistent, his tongue gently driving into my mouth.

He sets me down, turning me so I'm on my stomach then grabs my hips and lifts me up, pulling my ass to him. His stiff rod pushes between my cheeks, pressing up against my virgin hole.

A thrill tinged with fear races through me, then impulsively I push against his hard cock.

My tightest hole resists, unwilling to give, but I keep pressing, not forcing but encouraging.

Shen and Alaric move around the bed, then climb on so they're both next to my head with their large rods bouncing in my face.

Grabbing them both, I steady myself with their dicks, then continue my intention to take Tynan fully in.

The pressure builds, but it isn't painful so much as intense. Magic flows to the area, and the muscles relax as my intention takes hold through its very nature. There's a popping sensation, then he's inside of me.

"Ah!" I cry out more in surprise than pain or discomfort.

The sensation of fullness there is different, new, but also pleasurable. My eyes roll up into my head, and I groan louder as he slowly, oh so slowly, inserts himself fully into my ass.

Shen and Alaric lean down, kissing my cheeks, my neck, their hands run through my hair tugging and pulling.

Tynan holds his position, letting me adjust and grow used to it before he pulls back and gently pushes in and out.

"Yes," I groan, moaning as he fills me then retreats.

I pull Alaric into my mouth and slide down his cock to the hilt, licking it as I pull off, then do the same for Shen.

With each thrust in by Tynan I take one, then the other in my mouth, down to my throat and back out.

We work, back and forth, and as they take my body, I take their strength, pulling their magic into me. Our magics blend together, becoming something more and new, even as our bodies join.

I don't know how long we go on in this way, but it feels amazing. Finally, Tynan pulls out of my ass, and the other two move as well. I'm only partially sated, but I let him have control, knowing my pleasure is the singular goal of all three of them.

Tynan cleans himself before he lies down on the bed on his back, his cock standing erect and waiting. Shen has moved around behind me where he grabs my hips and lifts me up. He shifts me over and lowers me onto Tynan's erect dick until it's fully in my pussy.

Tynan's hands slide up my arms to tangle in my hair. Gently, he pulls me down, kissing me with a fiery passion so hot I'm surprised it doesn't burn.

Pressure is against my ass again, and surprise causes me to pull back from Tynan's kiss.

"Relax," he orders, and amazingly I do.

Now that I've had one dick in my ass, it's surprisingly

easy for Shen to slide in, even though Tynan is in my pussy too.

I thought I'd felt full before, but nothing can compare to this. Their hard rods rub against each other as they take turns pushing in, then out.

As I think I've reached my limit, Alaric takes hold of my chin and lifts my head up. As I meet his eyes, mouth opening in surprise, and he shoves his dick in.

All three of them thrust in and out as one unit. Pleasure, so intense, mounts and I can't contain it.

Each thrust they make into me, magic pumps along with it. I take them, accepting them, pulling on their strength and replenishing my own.

The joining goes to another level. Each thrust they make, I know them more. They're ancient, so old, even before they were marked to be horsemen, they roamed the earth. Dragons that were here before man, and certain they will be here long after we are gone.

The magical field fills me, bringing more of their memories and thoughts with it as our energies come into alignment.

Memories of their hunts together. The conquests they've known. Dimly a memory of when they were marked as the Horsemen of the Apocalypse.

Along with that memory comes a blindingly bright, golden-white symbol. It's intricate, so intricate it's almost hypnotic as I see it with the eyes of magical awareness. This is their mark. I saw it, briefly, when I was first with Tynan, but then I was too carried away with the pleasure to really study it.

This time there are two of them, not three. Studying the pattern, it almost makes sense, but something is wrong with it, off in some mystical manner. There, when they shift from one design to the next, there's an echo left behind. It only lasts a moment, but it's clearly there. Now that I've spotted it, I can't miss it. It's a shadow of the symbol itself. Their marks have been corrupted by the shadow forces.

As I stare at them, three men taking my body, our magic melding, an idea occurs to me.

As they flow power to me, I shape it and then flow it at the symbols.

They all moan, loudly, so loud it pulls my attention to our bodies joining. In that instant the sensations overwhelm me, and I explode with pleasure and magic.

It rips through me and out at the same time. Moving in a concentric wave out of my core, my body tightening and arching, toes curling as I cry aloud with the intensity of the sensations.

Magic flows out of me in a torrent. I'm not only recharged, I'm overcharged. I've got more than I can possibly contain so it explodes out, racing through them.

I see their symbols, and they dissolve under the onslaught of my power. I know it, and I know this is the right thing. I set them free even as they sate the desires of my body.

As it rages, I rise above the storm of magic. I'm standing on a pinnacle in the raging force of our combined energies. It's a flow, it's wild but tamable, and as I see it rushes to obey. It obeys me, follows my orders, fulfills my needs.

I'm closer to who I'm meant to be, I'm becoming more than I was, and while I know it's not complete, I'm further along than I've been.

Expended, all of us collapse on the bed together, breathing heavily. Soft touches and kisses as the last remnants of our pleasure race through our bodies, and then, almost as one, we fall asleep entangled with each other.

Dark, cloying shadows surround me as I wander a wasted landscape.

Something is chasing me. No, not something, some things. Lots of them. Shadowy shapes with glowing eyes and evil intentions racing towards me causing the shadows themselves to be sticky and thick.

I try to run but it's impossible. I can't move faster no matter how I try.

I reach for my magic, intending to burn away the shadows with its light, and only a trickle responds to my call.

I glance over my shoulder, and fear grips me so tight I'm almost ready to give up, but the will to fight surges up and I run.

I know they're getting closer. Feel them breathing down my neck.

When I glance back, claws of darkness swipe out of the shadows, and I duck. Red eyes glow with fiery hate as another set of claws swings. Ducking, I trip and roll, coming to a stop on my knees.

Where is everyone? Why am I alone?

I leap to my feet, but before I can run again, I'm surrounded. I can't see them directly, but I know they're there in the shadows moving in on me.

"Tynan! Shen! Alaric!" I scream their names, terror rising and closing my throat as the last syllable slips out.

More claws swing, and trails of smoke linger in the air where they pass as I dodge.

They appear around me. The Dragons are next to me, each of them facing out. Their aspects shimmer, and they take on draconic imagery. They breathe fire, and the deep shadows retreat then rush back in as the flames fade.

At their presence, the connection to my magic opens again and I step up beside them, facing it with them. Claws swing in and grab my right arm.

"Ah!" I scream, as it burns into my flesh, then my magical defenses kick in, and the hand gripping me disintegrates into nothingness.

Smiling, I look out at the encroaching shadows. Confidence fills me, and I know what I have to do.

"Not this time," I say, and throw my arms wide, magic blasts out of me blindingly white chasing all the shadows away.

I awake with a start, sitting upright.

The three men are instantly alert, and all of them reach for and touch me.

"Ow," I exclaim.

"Aviella," Tynan says, his voice soft.

On my arm where he just touched me is a burn mark that looks like four elongated fingers. The three men look at it and none of us say a word, but we all know. The Shadow Forces are moving.

CHAPTER THIRTEEN

AVIELLA

"How's your focus now?" Silas asks, taking a break from putting me through my paces.

"It's better," I acknowledge, gratefully sitting down and wiping sweat from my forehead.

He pushes me to the limits of what I can do with my magic, and it's more exhausting than I would think.

"Good," he says, staring.

Leaning back in the chair, I sip a lemonade until his constant stare becomes annoying.

"What?" I ask.

He grimaces, opens his mouth to say something, then snaps it shut and shakes his head.

"It's nothing," he says, rising to his feet. "Let's continue."

"No," I say, setting down my drink. "Say it. You've been giving me odd looks all day. What is it?"

"After our, joining, you and I are connected," he says, not looking directly at me.

"Right," I agree, waiting for him to make his point. He doesn't say anything, waiting while I think it through. "Oh..."

It dawns on me what he means. He felt it when I... oh,

god. My cheeks burn like an inferno. Now I can't meet his eyes, not that he's looking directly at me either.

This is exactly the kind of thing I was worried about if I slept with any of my protectors. One or the other of them would be hurt, and I don't want to hurt any of them. They're all too important to me for that.

"I..." that's all the words I have.

My mind is blank, empty of thought, all I've got is feeling on the spot and embarrassed at the same time. What do I say? Sorry I didn't invite you too? That makes me snort, and Silas looks for the first time.

Something on his face or the absurdity of the situation, I don't know, but now I'm laughing. There's almost a hysterical edge to it. Oh god, what am I doing?

"Aviella," he says turning to me. "It's fine. There is no commitment."

I can't stop laughing. When I look at him it's even funnier. Except it's not, but what do I do with any of this? Heart racing, skin flushing, I laugh. Silas stares at me for a long, awkward moment, then he chuckles, and in moments he's laughing too.

"I'm sorry," I gasp for air between more bouts of laughter.

"Yeah," he says, shaking his head and wiping away tears.

"This entire thing is... weird," I say. "There's no playbook for it."

He grows somber and nods.

"You're right," he says. "and it's obvious that your power is not only growing with your... joinings... but your control is as well."

"I feel that too," I say. "I've always felt connected to you and them, but now it's so much more."

He nods. "I'd like to do some blood tests now. I have some new ideas."

"Sure," I agree. "What's that going to show that all the magical scans haven't?"

"Tynan and I were discussing it, and he had an idea of how to do a magical scan on your blood itself."

"Oh," I say. "Sounds crazy."

"It is," he agrees, surprising me. "But it might work, and nothing else so far has."

"Well," I say. "Guess we're at that point we have to do what we have to do. I'm not going to wait much longer."

"I think we're all well aware of that," he smiles.

"Let's get this over with," I say.

Nodding, he leads the way into his workspace and directs me to sit on a stool. A quick swab with a ball of cotton, then he sticks a needle into me and draws my blood. He's surprisingly skillful, and it really is no more than a pinch.

As if on cue, Tynan sweeps into the work area unannounced. He smiles when he sees me, his eyes burning with fiery passion.

"Aviella," he says, and his voice is sultry, like silk across my skin.

"Tynan," I greet him, suppressing a shiver.

Silas looks between the two of us, grimaces, then addresses Tynan.

"Where are your brothers?" Silas asks.

"They'll be here shortly," Tynan answers, never taking his eyes off me.

Silas grunts then returns to his work. Tynan and I stare at each other, his passion a physical force pressing against my skin. Before I'd slept with him, I thought he oozed sex, but it's so much more. His passion is primal, raw, with more depth and layers than any human I've ever met. Everything he does, all his thoughts, are filled with it.

"I've got it," Silas says causing Tynan and me to break our staring contest.

"Have you?" Tynan asks.

"Yeah," Silas says holding up a vial. "I've separated it enough that I think the magical scan will reveal more than we've been able to find so far."

The door opens and Shen and Alaric stalk into the room. Every ounce the predators, they don't have the refinement that Tynan cultivates. They are on the hunt, always, and that flows from them.

When they look at me each of them has a knowing smile but behind that I feel their desire. They're enamored with me and they can try to hide it if they want, but I know. They're mine.

A smile forms on my lips as I realize the depths of what that means. Me. An orphan girl has three dragons bound to her in such a way they'll do anything for me.

"Glad you made it," Silas say, an unusual hint of snark to his voice.

"Glad to help," Shen says, smiling at me and winking.

Silas directs the dragons into position and then gives them instructions for what they're supposed to do. As they set about the work the magic rises in the room making the hair on my arms stand on end.

They stare at the vial that now floats in the air between them, each flowing their own unique magics into the ounce of my blood.

Symbols appear in the air around it, shifting, changing symbols one fading into the next.

"What is that?" I exhale.

The symbols are made of a goldish light. They're beautiful to look at, artistry in motion as they shift.

"That is your genetic line made manifest," Silas explains, pointing at the symbols. "Each generation going back is a unique symbol."

"Oh, so it's like DNA," I say.

"Yes and no, this shows more than any scientist ever unlocked with DNA."

"There," Alaric says, pointing to the latest symbol to have formed in the air.

"Yes," Shen says, nodding appreciatively.

"We've seen that," Tynan says, thoughtful.

"The Euricyes papers?" Shen asks.

"No, I think not, I think it's the Eridisean remnants," Alaric answers.

"Enheduanna's writings," Tynan says, certainty in his voice. "Yes, this was in his writings."

"Enhe-who?" I ask.

Tynan smiles then reaches out and grabs the vial of my blood from where it hangs in the air between the dragons, handing it back to Silas.

"Enheduanna," Tynan says, saying the name slowly. "An ancient Sumerian philosopher."

"He was what, twenty-three, twenty-four centuries before the common era?" Alaric asks.

"As I recall, yes," Silas says.

I stare at the four men in utter disbelief. The crazy things is, they're serious. They are talking about a guy who lived forty or fifty centuries ago as if they knew him. Which leads me to having to ask.

"Did you... know him?" I ask, looking at each of them in turn.

"Personally?" Tynan asks, arching an eyebrow. "No, I took little interest in the humans at that time."

"Yes," Silas says. "He was an interesting fellow, bit of a drunk, but insightful."

And here I thought my world couldn't get any weirder.

"Talk about robbing the cradle," I snort, unable to resist popping the joke off.

All four of them look at each other in either disbelief or non-comprehension.

"Right," Tynan says. "Let's get those papers."

"I'll get them," Shen offers, moving out of the room with blurring speed.

Having the three men in the same room is awkward. It's worse because I'm aware of each of their emotional states through my connection to them.

The three dragons are comfortable with each other and are, apparently, used to sharing. Silas is a different matter. Despite the methuselah's extreme age, it's clear to me that he's never been one for sharing.

He's uncomfortable knowing what happened between the three dragons and me, and unsure where he fits into the equation. He'd never say it out loud or admit it if asked, but he can't completely block me.

Strangely, for me, it's comfortable. As I've come to accept my feelings for each of them, I've grown stronger. My connection to each is strong and only made stronger by our joining physically. Inside I feel a remarkable balance, as if I'm being lifted by them, their energy expanding and multiplying my own.

Thoughts of how to keep balance, not only in my life, but among the men I care about swirl through my head. My balance alone isn't all that matters.

Tynan comes in close, then suddenly he grabs me by my hips, spins me into him, and his lips are on mine. Surprised, I return the kiss as his tongue drives into my mouth, claiming it. He grinds his hips and his magic pours into me, bringing his fiery passion with it.

My body responds and there's no stopping it. Groaning, desire and need pushing to the front, I grab his hair and hold him tight against me, unwilling to break the kiss.

The demand for air finally supersedes all other desire,

and he breaks the kiss. I'm left panting, shaking with the intensity of it all. His eyes hold mine, the fire in them a pool of dancing flames that I want to dive into and lose myself.

Heart racing, I tear my eyes from his as awareness of where I am and who I'm with returns with a crash. Silas is pointedly not looking in my direction. Tynan has a devilish grin on his face.

Jerk, he did that on purpose. Rolling my eyes, I push him away and move across the room, imposing space between us to exert some control. Shen's return is perfectly timed and gives us all something else to focus on besides the rising testosterone. Shen stops, looks at each person in turn, then a slow grin spreads across his face and he chuckles.

"Already?" he asks.

Alaric snorts before bursting into laughter. Silas stares at the ground as if he might burn his way into it.

"You have them?" Tynan asks, the only one of us unperturbed by anything, apparently.

"Of course," Shen says, waving a stack of yellowed papers in his hand.

He lays them out on one of Silas's work tables. They're so ancient the edges are crumbling. I'm afraid to even touch them they look so delicate. They look like they're pages of a book that have been torn from their home. Staring at them and the strange symbols covering them, I can almost read them.

Almost, but not actually. Frowning, I glare at them and try to make the nebulous concepts form into words, but it doesn't work. I grit my teeth and rub my eyes.

"Interesting," Silas says, poring over them.

"Indeed," Tynan agrees.

"What?" I ask, my voice a bit too sharp.

Silas continues poring over the papers without bothering to look up. Tynan moves to a stool and takes a seat, casual yet sophisticated as ever. Only Tynan could make such a simple thing as taking a seat an exercise in seduction.

I don't know how he does it, but my body responds involuntarily, desire burning through my veins instantly. It's not missed by any of the men present either. Each of them glance in his direction, and I notice Silas's grimace before he returns his attention to the papers.

"It would make sense," Silas mutters.

"I agree," Shen says, straightening from his own study of the papers.

"Great, is anyone going to actually tell me what they say?" I snap.

"Of course," Tynan says. "They're a prophecy, of sorts. On their own, they don't mean much. History is filled with prophecies, and anyone with a bit of clever application can make them fit anything, but what these do that's different is they establish a theme."

"Right," I nod. "A theme. Great. Tells me absolutely nothing, thanks for that by the way. Now, what does that mean?"

Tynan arches an eyebrow at my snark. Magic crackles through the room as my irritation edges towards anger. The four men stop what they're doing.

"Aviella," Silas says, his voice soft and calm.

"What? Do you all think I have time for this? Have you forgotten that my dad is out there, captured, being tortured?

"I've had enough of waiting! No more games, no more word play, someone tell me what the hell these papers say and why they matter!"

My magic rolls across my skin, crackling the air, blue sparks falling off of me as it continues to build. No one says a word, but each of them take a step back, and I feel them raise their magical shields.

"Well enough," Tynan says, rising from his stool. Bold, without a hint of fear, he crosses the room and takes my hands in his. Warmth flows from them into me. "Allow us to explain."

"Okay," I agree, forcing my magic back under control.

"You are, of course, familiar with the Christian beliefs?" he asks, still holding my hands.

"Sure," I say. "Dad educated me into it."

"Good, then you know of the Christ and his twelve disciples?" I nod along with his words. "As with so much of the Judeo-Christian belief, this theme is echoed through history."

"Are you saying they borrowed it from earlier religions?" I ask, disbelieving his words.

"No," he shakes his head. "I'm saying that human history has worked in patterns. Things repeat. He was not the first, and he was not the last."

"I don't get it," I answer, trying to wrap my head around the concept.

"It's not an easy thing to grasp, that's fine," he says, tightening his grip on my hands. "We see it easier because, well bluntly, we've witnessed it first hand through untold ages."

"Right, you're all older than dirt," I say, laughing as that idea really hits him. "Cradle robbers."

Tynan's eyes widen then he bursts into unexpected laughter. It's only a moment before Shen, Alaric, and even Silas are laughing too. It's a needed break from the previous tension.

"I suppose we are," Tynan says, trailing a finger along my jaw to my chin. He pulls it away before it becomes too much.

"Ok, so what does it all mean?" I ask, returning to the case in point. "I'm certain you have a point to make."

"I do," Tynan smiles, returning to his stool. "The story of the one with twelve isn't a new one. It's a repeating pattern, one that has happened more than once in history."

"Oh," I say, an idea begins to form.

Twelve. Efram, Rafe, Nathaniel, Silas, Tynan, Shen, Alaric, Ronan, Killian, Luca, Gavin, and...?

Tynan smiles, a knowing look on his face.

"Thirteen is a mystical number," he continues. "In your 'modern' times it has connotations of being unlucky with various superstitions surrounding it and its use. That's not true throughout history. It's a powerful number. Often you'll find covens are capped at thirteen."

"Thirteen," I say, turning the idea over in my head.

Each of the men in my life, the connection I've felt to them, the drawing together and the, being honest, almost irresistible desire for each of them.

I've never been 'that' kind of girl, whatever the hell that means. I do know that I never, in my wildest fantasies, ever thought I could feel this way about more than one man. Truth is though, I do.

"It ties to your fate, Aviella," Silas says, speaking for the first time.

"Yeah," I say, shaking my head. "Okay."

What else do I say? What do I do?

"Let's be blunt," Tynan says. "Perhaps you are familiar with the *Da Vinci Code*?"

"No," I answer, confused. "Isn't that an old movie or something? I was like six when the Apocalypse happened."

Tynan grimaces. "I do forget how young you are. Yes, it was a movie and a book."

"Okay, what's that got to do with anything?" I ask.

Tynan looks at the other men, and almost as one they nod.

"You're a direct descendant of the line of Mary Magdalene," Tynan says.

"Who?" I ask, confused but a warm glow suffuses me and everything takes on a golden aura.

"The wife of Jesus, who in turn is of the line tracing its way back to Inanna," Silas says.

"And Inanna was?" I ask.

"A Sumerian goddess of love and war," Silas answers. "At least she is recalled as such, but the stories of her also speak of her twelve."

"Oh," I say, power building inside that I don't think I can contain much longer.

"It brings a new understanding to everything," Alaric says.

"But it doesn't bring us any closer to freeing my dad," I answer, the golden auras tinging with red as anger comes along with the building energy.

"We'll find him soon," Tynan says, making a motion with his hand.

The gesture is dismissive and pisses me off. The anger bubbles over.

"I think--" I start to say, but my words are cut off as it bursts out of me, creating a shockwave of force. Blasting out in a concentric circle around me, my men and anything not nailed down is thrown back against the walls.

"We need to find him," I finish, then collapse to my knees.

Slowly I climb back to my feet as each of my men rise, dusting themselves off. No one says anything for a long moment that stretches way past the point of being awkward.

"Sorry," I say when no one says anything. I am sorry, mostly. "Look, this is all... great. Whatever, fine. I'm sure it's helpful, but there's one thing that matters to me most. Finding my dad. He's in trouble, and I have to save him. First and foremost."

Staring them down, hands on my hips, I lock eyes with each one of them in turn, and as I do, each of them nods.

"We understand, Aviella," Tynan says.

"Good," I say. "We have to find him, fast. Then we'll figure out how to save the world."

None of them argue or say anything further, so I spin on my heel and march out of the room. I'm not sure if that went well or terrible.

In the halls, heading for the upper floors where my rooms are, people move out of my way on their own. I'm halfway to my goal when I actually notice it, because a young couple races to the opposite side of the hall and casts wary looks at me as they pass.

What now? I wonder.

It keeps happening until I'm locked in my rooms, alone and glad for the quiet. Walking to the bedroom to change into something more comfortable, I catch a glimpse of myself in one of the full-length mirrors. A bright, white glow surrounds me.

"You've got to be kidding me," I say, shaking my head. "I'm a walking light bulb!"

One of the guys could have said something. What do I do with this?

I focus on my image in the mirror and try to will the light to go away, but that only makes it glow brighter until the reflection of it is damn-near blinding.

"Gah!" I exclaim, throwing my arms up in the air. "Screw it."

Throwing myself on the bed, I wrap my arm around the pillow and close my eyes. Thoughts of my dad circle around and around until I fall into sleep's welcome embrace.

SWIRLING SHADOWS COVER THE BLASTED LANDSCAPE. STRANGE. When I lift my hand it's thin, see-through, and almost misty on its own. This is a dream, it has to be.

A bright, white beacon flares up on the horizon, pulling my attention to it. It's my dad. I know it with all the certainty I know who I am.

In that direction, I flow along the ground that is pock-marked with craters from the wars. Swirling shadows grow thicker as I pass, but I ignore them.

"Dad!" I scream. "I'm coming."

There's no answer, of course, why would there be? It doesn't matter. Movement here corresponds to thought, so I will myself to go faster.

Ahead there's a wall of blackness growing larger as I approach until it looks to stretch for as far as I can see in either direction and hundreds of feet into the air.

I clench my fists and summon my magic. It forms a white ball of crackling energy around my hand. A grin narrows my eyes and lights up my face.

"Bring it," I taunt the blackness, coming to a stop before the wall.

It pulses, throbbing like a slow beating heart, then the wall undulates and spits forth its minions.

Creatures of nightmare, birthing out with terrifying screeches echoed by the screams of damned souls. The white ball of magic flickers, it's an instant as a shred of doubt crosses my thoughts, but I steel my resolve.

"No," I exhale, bolstering my nerves with anger.

Thousands of the things fill the air. Some flying, some crawling things that barely have limbs. All the monstrosities have teeth. So many sharp, nasty teeth, and they fill the air with their hunger.

They close around and the battle is joined. I fight with magic and fists. Utilizing every weapon, every move that my mentors have taught me. This is all that stands between my father and me. I will not be stopped!

Punching one thing in the face leaves me open for another to bite down on my shoulder. I'm screaming in pain as my entire right side goes numb, and black veins race through the white light of my magic.

It's too much. They're everywhere. Every time I drop one, four more take its place.

I'm going to lose.

My certainty wavers, hindered by the moment of doubt. The white light flickers, blinking out completely for a moment before struggling to return.

Desperation sets in, and now I'm fighting for my own survival.

A roar echoes over the munching, crunching sounds of the monsters. My ears ring at its force and my heart leaps into a new level of speed.

Sparing a glance up I see a dragon so black it stands out against the blackness of the sky it flies across. It roars again and the sound of it pounds against my chest. The creatures hesitate, looking up, and I sense their fear, but they renew their attacks with an intensified ferocity.

The world around me turns red and yellow. I throw my arms up to protect my eyes, and waves of heat pass over me again and again. Dying screams echo around me, and I'm forced to my knees, covering my head protectively.

A moment, then two, and I'm no longer being pounded on by hundreds of monstrous arms. When I glance out past my arm, the field around me is littered with the corpses of my attackers. Rising to my feet and turning a circle, I see thousands of them lying dead. The black wall has retreated, not gone, but further away and no longer giving rise to more monsters.

Tynan swaggers through the death and destruction up to me.

"Come," he says, grabbing my hand. "Before they gather a real force."

"No!" I yell, jerking my hand free. "My dad is over there! I have to get to him."

Tynan follows my pointing arm to the white beacon.

"Aviella," he says. "You're here to liberate the souls of the world. These sorts of things come with sacrifice. I will help you find him to the best of my ability, when the time is right. You must master yourself now, though. Don't let the power go to your head. You're not ready for this fight."

The bluntness combines with my knowing he's being honest. It cuts through the building rage in my heart.

"He's so close," I say.

"I know, but it's a trap," he says, taking my hand again. "Come, let's get out of this dreamscape."

He pulls me away and I let him take me away, only glancing over my shoulder once at the bright white beacon.

When I wake up, alone in my bed, my pillow is soaked with tears.

CHAPTER FOURTEEN

AVIELLA

*L*ast night was one long bout of tossing and turning. I don't think I ever truly slept, not after my dream walk. If Tynan hadn't found me when he did, I'd be dead. I know it and I hate it.

If I'm so all-flipping-powerful and fated to save the world, then why in the name of all that's holy can't I save my dad?

That single, burning question kept me up the rest of the night. When I finally gave up on sleeping, I came down to the lower levels to see if I could help out in the makeshift hospital. I've been healing various wounds and illnesses for a couple of hours now. It's something to pass the time and it makes me feel less useless.

"Thank you," the mother of the son says as I finish with her boy.

He'd manage to give himself a nasty cut that would have taken stitches and a couple of weeks to heal, if they managed to not let it get infected, which isn't an easy thing in its own right.

"It's nothing," I answer, wiping sweat from my brow.

"I can't... pay you but," tears fall from her eyes. "I will never forget you. Maybe someday I can help you in return." She grips my arm tightly so I cover her hand with my own, smiling.

"Seriously, I should be thanking you. I'm glad to help," I reassure her.

She gathers her boy and carries him off, and I look through the curtain of my area for the next patient. Efram is standing there as if waiting on me.

"Hi," he says, a smile on his face.

"Hey," I say.

"This isn't a great idea," he says, motioning around.

"Why not?" I snap. "I'm not a little bird to sit in my gilded cage ready to 'sing' for you and everyone else!"

He holds his hands up in front of us, making calming motions, his cheeks flushing bright red.

"That's not—" he starts.

"I don't care what you meant," I huff, stepping back into the exam space and taking a seat on the bed.

Hanging my head, I roll my shoulders and suppress a yawn.

"What's wrong?" Efram asks, pulling a stool close and sitting.

"I'm tired," I say, staring at the stone floor.

"I got that," he answers. "And?"

Looking up, I shake my head. I'm too tired to keep it up, so I let it drop again and my shoulders slump along with it. Now I can't hide the yawn.

Efram places a gentle hand on my shoulder and then stands up and moves behind me. He massages the knots he finds there, and I groan as he finds the particularly sore spots.

"I didn't sleep much last night," I say at last.

"Nightmares?" he asks, understanding.

"You could say that," I say, not wanting to go into details on what happened.

There's enough tension already between Efram and the others. He's such a gentle soul compared to the others. In some ways he's the one I'm closest to, if that's because I've known him the longest, or only the nature of what we are, I don't know.

He continues massaging my shoulders, kneading the muscles until my neck cracks loudly.

"Better?" he asks.

"Yeah, thanks," I answer, rolling my head and shoulders in a circle.

"Come on, let's get out of here," he says.

"Fine," I agree, feeling satisfied that I've done enough for the day.

The exhaustion lying on me like a two-ton weight absolutely factors into my agreement, even though I know he has some purpose he's not telling me. Suppressing yet another yawn, I follow him out and into the halls.

I'm not at my most alert, so we travel quite a way before it strikes me that we're traveling down, not up towards my quarters.

"Where are we going?" I ask.

Efram pauses to look at me.

"I thought we'd go see Merrick," he says, a half-grin on his face.

"Why?" I ask, staring into his arresting silver-violet eyes.

He shakes his head, staring past me into the empty distance. He shrugs and changes directions heading for the upper floors.

I don't move, waiting until he turns back to me. A storm plays in those beautiful eyes, no matter that his face is carefully schooled into showing no emotion.

"Coming?" he asks.

"Efram," I say, a pleading note in my voice. "Talk to me. Please."

A fire ignites in his eyes as his body stiffens. He doesn't speak, standing stock-still, staring. I wait him out. I have guesses at what is happening with him, but guesses are not his words. I want, no I need his words. Need him to talk to me.

When he still doesn't speak, I close the space between us, taking his hands in mine. Meeting his eyes, I squeeze his hands, and smile.

"Hey," I say.

"I'm sorry," he says.

"For what? You've done nothing wrong," I say.

He forces a smile that is more of a twitching of the corners of his mouth.

"Yeah," he says, shaking his head again. "Let's get you home."

"No," I say, tightening my grip on his hands so he can't pull away.

Reaching out with my magic I embrace him with it, surrounding him with energy.

"Aviella," he protests, but his magic intertwines with mine.

"Efram," I answer.

"This isn't safe," he says, but he makes no effort to move away.

"No, it's not," I agree, moving even closer, barely an inch separates our bodies, the tension rising in my own is reciprocated by his. "Talk to me."

Thoughts play behind his eyes. I know I've hurt him, but the only way to fix this is for us to confront it, head on.

"I've missed you," he says.

"I've missed you, too," I smile. "A lot."

"Things are changing," he says.

"As they do," I agree.

He's dancing around what he wants to say, or maybe do, but it's okay. I want him to take the lead. Letting go of one his hands, I touch his chest, and let my fingers trail down.

He grabs me, roughly, pulling me against him, then pushing me against the wall. His lips smash into mine, claiming me even as I welcome him.

The passion of his kiss is incomparable. Thoughts are blasted away. His lips moving against mine are everything, pulling all my attention. Only dimly am I aware of his bulge digging into my stomach, his hips grinding against me, his hands roaming up and down my sides.

His magic is the waves of the ocean, pounding against a cliff wall that is me. Beating, thrumming, humming with an energy that is uniquely him.

Opening myself to him, I pull his magic in, taking it, claiming him through it. New channels form as the two different energies combine into something new.

"Aviella," he growls, momentarily breaking the kiss to let us both breathe.

It's not enough though, I want more, need more from him. Grabbing his head, I pull him down and continue our kiss. Drinking him in, magically and physically.

His hands are on my ass, pulling me into his groin, our bodies writhe together and any moment we'll be joining. Fleetingly I think about where we are but I don't care. Desire and need outweigh any considerations of propriety.

His energy is ethereal, penetrating me in ways that none of the others have. He's air and I'm a drowning woman, needing his life-giving breath.

The strength of his body and his magic support me as I give myself. Our kiss continues until at last he breaks again, one arm against the wall, his forehead resting on mine. We're breathing heavily, letting the moment stretch.

"I don't want to see Merrick," I say, fingers resting on his beautifully sexy jawline. "Let's go, tea, coffee, cards, just the two of us, okay?"

He hesitates, and though he never physically moves, I sense his withdrawal. It's slight but unmistakable.

"Yes," he says, nodding, then planting a loving, tender kiss on my forehead.

He takes my hand, and now I lead the way, heading for my rooms in the upper level. The guards to the upper levels give us a dirty look, but they know better than to try and interfere with me. I know, beyond a shadow of a doubt though, that Tynan will know Efram and I are together and in my rooms. Let him know. It doesn't matter.

If their great prophecy about me is true, I need all twelve of my men. Maybe that's a justification in my mind, but more important, I think it's a justification in their minds. I've known for a while what my heart wanted. I couldn't wrap my head around it or see any way to make it work here in reality, even in the reality of the Apocalypse in which we all find ourselves. The prophecy though, maybe?

Right now none of that matters. My chest swells as we walk along, and I'm walking on air. I didn't realize how much I've missed Efram. Sure, we see each other all the time, but seeing each other isn't the same as the quiet times we've had. The long nights talking, passing the time together.

Each of the guys brings something unique, but of all of them Efram is the one I still feel closest to. The connection between us is different and, in some ways, more than anything I have with the others.

"Drink?" I ask, moving to the small kitchenette that is part of my suite of rooms.

"Tea?" he asks.

"Sure," I say, putting on the kettle.

He takes a seat and waits while I prepare tea, then we settle in, each with our cups, and sit.

"It's been a long while since we've done this," he observes.

"Yeah," I say. "I miss it."

"Tynan likes to keep you locked away," he says, storm clouds passing behind his eyes.

"Tynan is Tynan," I say, dismissively, but I know he knows.

I'm not sure how, probably Tynan bragging, knowing him, but Efram knows I've slept with Tynan. Does he know about the others too?

Sipping my tea, I cover my staring as I try to read his magical aura. He's in turmoil and it shows. Colors swirl around him, but outside he's my dear, sweet, stoic Efram. There's pain he carries, and instinctively I want to take it from him.

"Efram," I say, following a hunch. "Tell me about before."

"Before?" he asks, surprise in his face and voice.

"Before the Apocalypse, before... all of this. What was your life like? Tell me, please."

He sips some tea, looking thoughtful. I've always known there was a loss in his past, a hole in his heart, it's an ache in him that he mostly ignores. Focusing on it, I want to know, need him to share it with me.

"I lived in New York City," he says. "When the world came down."

"Oh," I say, encouraging him to continue.

He stares into his cup of tea, his features taking on a faraway look. The corners of his lips curl, only slightly, as if the hint of a smile is weighed down by the memories.

"You probably don't know what it was like, being magical before the Apocalypse hit. We hid our true nature in the 'normal' world," he laughs. "I worked in the coroner's office."

I snort, spewing tea, unable to hold back my own laughter.

"I guess that makes sense," I say, grabbing a towel and dabbing at my shirt.

"Yeah," he says. "My talents were useful there, I helped the dead to cross over, delivered last messages occasionally, things like that."

"Were you... alone? Did you have anyone?" I probe.

"Yes," he says, falling silent.

"Efram?" I ask, reaching across the space between us and resting my hand on his.

His skin is warm, the warmth of him flows in through that singular point of contact. It's so different with him. He's every bit as passionate as Tynan or Silas, but his passion is different. Almost more mature?

"My sister," he says, and I recall he's mentioned her briefly before.

"What was she like?" I ask, pushing him towards pleasant memories.

His half-grin forms and his eyes light up.

"A joy," he sighs. "She loved... everything. She was an artist, painter, and she saw beauty in everything, even the end of the world didn't dim her vision."

"She sounds amazing," I say.

He opens himself to me in a way none of the others ever have. I see his sister, in his mind's eye, he doesn't lock me out or hold back, unlike the dragons or Silas. He welcomes me in and our magic intertwines in a way that is more intimate than if we were having sex.

She is beautiful, seeing her the way he saw her. She laughs easily and loves much. As he tells me about her, I see his memories of it.

"We were close," he says, finishing another story of their time together.

"What happened?" I ask, feeling the darkness waiting behind his last story.

"The Apocalypse," he snorts. "When the first seal was broken, New York was ground zero. I tried to get out of there with her. We didn't make it."

Power surges through him as he confronts the memory, but now, he's not alone. I'm there with him as it comes to the forefront. He tries to push it down, hide it as he has for years, but I grip his hand and flow my magic into him.

He stiffens, slightly, then together we face the memory. Him pulling her along as the streets of New York City are literally tearing themselves apart.

Demons crawling out of the crevasses, angels flying across the sky, the war of heaven come to earth. Confronted by a monstrosity, he pushed her behind him while he fought it, but he didn't see the one coming up that way.

Tears flow as I witness, with him, the loss. Our energies combine, and the pain of the memory fades, not becoming less, but not hurting him as much.

Relief floods his face and he lays his free hand over mine, clasping tightly. In the moment of silence between us, there's an awareness we're not alone. Frowning, not wanting to ruin this, I glance around without moving my head.

A shadowy figure stands to the left, and when I catch a full sight, it's clear that it's his sister. She's still with him.

'Efram, I forgive you,' she says, her voice a barren whisper.

He doesn't seem to hear her, strange, how is it I can and he doesn't?

"Efram," I say, he looks up, eyes wet with unshed tears. "She's here."

"No, she's gone," he says, shaking his head.

"No, she's here, she says she forgives you," I tell him, and as I do, I flow magic into him.

His power flows into me, joining, and once more new channels open. He follows my gaze and his eyes widen.

"Boo?" he asks.

The shimmery figure smiles and nods, reaching an ethereal hand towards him.

'I love you,' she says. 'Forgive yourself.'

Tears flow from all three of us but Efram nods then she brightens as if the sun is shining on her forming a bright halo around her. As the light fades, she goes with it and she's gone.

"Are you okay?" I ask, kneeling before him and wrapping my arms around him.

"Yes," he says. "Thank you."

We hold each other for a long time without the necessity of words. It's clear to me that Efram's and my relationship is fated to be different than all the others. Every bit as intertwined but it touches places in me that the others don't come close to. Perhaps that's why he's dragging things out. I still have a deep aching need for him, physically, but now, his energy pulses in mine, his abilities are mine too.

In time, we'll join fully. When the time is right for both of us. Until then, I'll enjoy what we have together.

CHAPTER FIFTEEN

AVIELLA

*E*fram takes his leave after a few more hours, and once more I'm left to my own devices. Obviously dream-walking on my own is a bad idea, so that's out. Out of sheer frustration and boredom I finally doze off sitting in a chair, obstinately reading a book.

A knock at the door jerks me out of a fitful sleep. I throw it open, my eyes bleary, and with a lethargy about my muscles, I stare at the ridiculous-looking person standing there.

"The Mighty Lords say, you need to play, your entertainment is their delight. Please come, dear chum. It will be fun, we're not a bum," the person, who I think might be male, says.

The effeminate man is wearing heavy layers of pancake make-up on his face and hands. Red rouge colors his cheeks, electric-blue eye shadow, ruby-red lips and nails painted coal black. A silk suit done in red with black trim and a white shirt. He dances from foot to foot as he sing-songs his terrible poetry.

"Huh?" I ask, thoughts thick with the fog of having just

been woken up.

"A celebration!" he exclaims, flourishing his arms wildly. "An entertainment. Throw decorum to the side, come alive!"

Irritation rising, I struggle to control my temper.

"Right," I frown. "What is it you want me to come to, and who is the invitation from?"

His smile is so broad, it looks like his head could flip back from it. He nods with enough enthusiasm, I'm amazed his neck doesn't break and drop his head to the floor.

"The mighty and glorious lords Shen and Alaric request you attend a circus arranged for your amusement!"

After closing my eyes, I take a deep breath, then let it out slowly. A circus, another distraction. Lovely.

The connection I have with them throbs, and I know that this is their doing. It's clearer than ever their intentions are good, if slightly misguided. They know I'm obsessing over heading out to find my father and are doing what they can to help.

On one hand, it does help. Anything to focus my attention on besides the fact I'm waiting while he's being tortured is almost a welcome distraction.

Almost, but there's part of me that is always aware that I'm waiting when I should be in action. After all, what's the point of all this power if I don't go out and kick some ass?

"Fine," I say. "Where?"

He gives directions in another round of sing-song bad rhymes, and I close the door, not waiting for him to say more. I hate being rude, but I've had enough of the theatrics.

Quickly, I change clothes then leave my rooms, glad he's not still standing there when I open the door.

The circus is set up in the same space I've been before, and I make my way to the same skybox to watch. When I arrive, no one else is there, which is surprising.

Feeling strangely alone, I take a seat close to the railing

and settle in to watch the show. It's already in progress, and the stands are filled with ooh-ing and ahh-ing people.

Dim memories of a circus my dad took me to come back as I watch, and it warms my heart. The 'animals' in this circus are not the normal fare though, but trumpet beasts instead of lions and elephants.

The animals are put through various stunts, which is impressive, since they each look like they could eat the audience without a second thought.

Still it pulls my attention away from the worries and stress. A series of clowns come out and do a routine that makes me laugh, and they're followed by a group of acrobats.

Suddenly a cold chill hits me so hard I look around for a source, but don't see anything. I rise to my feet and lean over the railing, looking, and move along it. Something is wrong. The hairs on my arms are standing on end as an electrical sensation builds. It's hard to breathe as a pressure builds in the air.

A loud pop is followed by screams. A massive, swirling purple-black portal opens on the arena floor, and dead things pour out of it like clowns from a car. Each of them bears the same shadow mark that haunts my dreams.

They tear into the crowd and the performers, causing a stampede as they try to get away. The trumpet beasts, left unattended, break free and add to the chaos.

"No!" I scream, rage pouring out of me.

Focusing my magical energy, I throw it at the portal, trying to close it and stop the influx of the shadow army. Something fights me, and I pour more into it, digging deeper.

Struggling, I reach for more power and find the dragons' pools, and I suck them in, but still it's not enough. Something is holding that portal open.

I have an awareness it's a single being doing it. A thing of such powerful magnitude it's resisting my onslaught.

More, I need more power.

Screams punctuate my thought, and I stretch for more, pulling Silas's power, then at last Efram's.

"I. Will. Beat. You," I force the words out through gritted teeth, holding my arms out to focus the power, pushing my hands together in a closing motion.

It snaps shut, but there's a blast of air as it does, throwing undead monstrosities and the surviving members of the crowd forward. They tumble head over heels as the wave passes through them.

It's a momentary respite that passes too fast as the undead things grab for any living flesh and make a feast of it. Blinding rage wells up inside of me, and without another thought, I leap over the railing, falling towards the ground.

Focusing magic, I create gusts of wind that slow my descent so that I land lightly in the middle of the arena. The largest of the things is right ahead of me. A conjugation of human and monster parts, it's eight feet tall with four arms, eight mouths full of teeth, and two massive legs that shake the ground as it walks.

"Come at me," I yell, running right at it.

I've trained for this. I'm ready.

Undead hands reach for me as I run, but I'm quick on my feet, dodging from side to side.

A few feet before I reach the monster, I leap into the air, focusing all my magic around my left hand which I hold out in front of me, palm out.

My hand glows a brilliant, blinding white. My leap arcs me towards the thing. It moves, slower than me, arms coming up with two massive clubs swinging towards me.

"Ahhhh!" a wordless battle-cry gives sound to my boiling rage.

As I descend its mouths snap, saliva and ooze hanging as each of them struggle to take a bite of my flesh.

My hand lands on the swirling shadow mark on its head and the world explodes around me.

Fire and shadow blend with a flash of white. A fresh wave of force sends me tumbling head over heels through the air.

Landing in a heap, wind knocked out of my lungs, I force myself to roll over onto an elbow. Unable to inhale, my lungs scream and panic tries to set in.

No. Control, Aviella.

Spasms rock my body, but support comes from my men, their magic flowing through me, healing my broken ribs and giving me the gift of breath.

Lifting my head, I see my men arrive at that very moment. They fight the undead with their magics, working in unison as if a single, trained unit.

It's a beautiful thing to watch.

No differences, no petty arguments. My men, attacking the darkness—and they're winning.

Exhaustion hits me so hard, it's a massive effort of will to climb to my feet.

Forcing myself up, I join the fight, and it doesn't take long before we finish off the last of the dead things.

"Aviella," Tynan says, reaching me first.

He grabs my shoulders and steadies me as I waver on my feet. As I look around, my stomach turns sour, and bile rises in my throat. Hundreds of dead lie around us in a macabre display of carnage.

"So many," I say, tears rolling down my face.

Efram, Silas, Shen, and Alaric join Tynan, crowding around me, their energy and their arms supporting me.

No one speaks. What can they say? I feel their emotions the same as my own. We stand with each other for only a minute or two, then I push off of them.

Wispy, ethereal shapes hang over several of the bodies.

"Oh no," I say, looking at Efram.

"You see them?" he asks, surprise on his face and in his eyes.

"Yes," I answer, my heart breaking.

Fresh tears stream down my face as the dragons and Silas look at each other, not understanding.

"She sees the lost souls," Efram says, his voice barely above a whisper. "She's gained necro-sight."

Silas' head jerks toward me, and his eyes are piercing. The three dragons nod as if not surprised by this development.

"I have to help them," I say, looking at them.

The shimmering outlines move in slow circles around their fallen bodies, not moving on. It feels wrong and unnatural.

"You're right," Efram agrees.

He takes my hand and leads me over to one of the spirits. Slowly it turns towards us, wide-eyed and open mouthed. It shimmers, emulating a shudder.

"Hello," Efram says to it, his voice calm and soothing. "Let me help."

"My family," the spirit says.

"Who are they?" Efram asks.

The spirit tells him their names. Efram assures it that he will pass along their love then suggest they look around for a white light or a door.

"I see it, over there," the spirit says.

"Good, walk to it, go in peace," Efram says.

I watch as the spirit walks to a space where I see nothing else, but when it arrives there, it disappears.

"Where did it go?" I ask.

"Crossing over," he says, resting his hand on my arm. "I don't know, exactly. I've tried getting information from

Nathaniel and Rafe, but they're very tight-lipped, if they know anything."

Emptiness wells in my stomach, a yawning void of absolute despair. I can't give in to that, I know, because too much depends on me.

These people depended on me too, whether they knew it or not. I'm the one supposed to save them, and there's no doubt in my mind, this attack was aimed at me.

All this death and destruction was only to try and get to me. Resolve forms under the blackness, overtaking it and pushing it back to the nothingness from which it comes.

"I'm going to kill the one who did this," I growl through gritted teeth.

The five men with me exchange a look, but no one puts forth any disagreement. Efram and I finish the grim work of helping the stuck souls to move on and when, at last, the space is empty except for the six of us, we gather.

The three dragons are unusually quiet, but their anger is palpable, especially Tynan's. This is his home, and an invasion of this nature and size is clearly a massive gall for home.

"This was more than a feint," Silas says, breaking the silence.

"Yes," Tynan agrees, his teeth gritted, and the word all but spit out of his mouth. "They grow bold."

He and his brother dragons look at each other, and then they each nod in turn.

"What?" I snap.

As one the three of them turn and look at me.

"We have preparations to make," Shen says.

"Yes, we must act quickly," Alaric adds.

"What are you talking about," I ask, focusing my attention on Tynan.

"Give us a little time," Tynan says. "Not long, I assure you."

"That's not an answer," I say.

"I do understand," Tynan says. "This has to be investigated. They should not have been able to open a portal into this bunker. Somehow, we've been compromised. Give me a day, please."

When he adds the please, I know how much he wants this. Please isn't a word that Tynan uses lightly. Before now I would have sworn the word didn't exist in his vocabulary.

"Okay," I agree, glancing over at Efram and Silas to see if they have any disagreements. "One day, then we meet to form an answer to this. I'm done with waiting."

No one has anything else to add, so the dragons take off, leaving me alone with Efram and Silas.

"Any word from Nate or Rafe?" I ask, but they shake their heads. "We're going to have to move soon. We can't keep waiting."

"I'll see if I can contact them," Silas says.

"Good," I answer.

"Let's get you back upstairs," Efram says. "It's more defensible there if we need it."

I let him lead me away, leaving everyone else to the work at hand. My nerves thrum with energy. There ought to be something I can do, but no matter what I think of on our long, silent walk, I reject it without voicing it.

The guards to the upper level let Efram pass, reluctantly, and only after I push them. Standing at my door, he holds my hands and we stare into each other's eyes. Impulsively, I wrap my arms around him and pull him tight against me, burying my face against his neck. Tears fall while he holds me, silent and strong. My beautiful, noble Efram.

The storm of emotions finally recedes, and he tells me goodnight, not once advancing anything. I watch him leave with a twinge of regret. It would be nice to not go to my bed alone, to have his strength to depend on while I try to sleep, but I can't ask that of him. No, with him at least, I'll move only when he's ready.

Closing my door behind me, I head straight for bed, physically and emotionally exhausted.

～

"AVIELLA, RUN!" DAD SCREAMS.

He's hanging from chains that bind his wrist and ankles, holding him at an angle. Blood drips from all over, disappearing below the swirling mist that forms the floor. Demonic red eyes glow from the shadows, and there's a constant chitter as of hundreds of rats.

"Daddy," I say, stumbling forward.

My limbs are heavy, as if the chains on him are weighing me down as well.

"Aviella, run, get out of here," he says, struggling against the chains.

"I'm coming!" I yell, running towards him.

A smoky shape forms next to him, red glowing mouths, it looks at me, opening a mouth to reveal a burning inferno inside. It laughs, a sound so chilling it slows my run forward. The air around me thickens making forward progress impossible.

A strong wind blows, forcing me back. I lean into it, digging my feet into the ground trying to push against it, but I can't.

Sliding back, I pull magic around me, forming a shield in front of myself. The wind breaks around the shield, but still I can't move forward.

The wind increases its force and no matter how I struggle, I continue to be pushed back, a foot at a time. Suddenly the wind stops, and I stumble forward almost falling on my face.

Now I'm outside a Bunker door. Rusted steel with two massive wheels and hinges that are almost as big as me.

My dad's in there, I have to get to him.

Pulling magic around my fists, I hit the door and there's a resounding echo, but the steel doesn't even dent a little. Raging, I hit it over and over, pouring all my anger and frustration into each resounding strike.

Nothing. It doesn't make a difference.

I turn and look over the empty plains. Everything is gloomy, overcast gray with streaks of red. Shadows swirl, almost forming shapes, before flitting away.

After walking a few feet away from the door, I take some time to look around. If I can figure out where I am then maybe, I'll know where we have to go to get him.

A mound of earth arcs over the door. In the far distance I see the bones of a ruined city. Former skyscrapers, now husks of the glorious buildings they once were, black claws scratching at the sky. There's not a single landmark I recognize.

I climb the hill to stand on top of the door to the Bunker. It gives me a better view, so I turn a slow circle. Something, anything that I can use to guide us to him.

The shadows thicken and the ground trembles. The air is suddenly cold, causing me to shiver.

"Aviella," my dad's voice calls. "Run, baby girl."

Something is wrong. Of course, there's something wrong, they've got my dad.

No. Something else. What is it?

A blackness hits me upside the head, and I'm knocked to the side, reeling. Pulling magic, I whirl to face it, but there's nothing there.

"He's mine," a female voice says, but I don't see the source. "You'll never get him. I'm having too much fun."

"Who are you!" I scream, turning circles as I try to spot the source.

Laughter echoes around me as another black streak hits me. Blood fills my mouth as stars explode in my head. I form magic into a shell around me. I'm being hit from all sides by shadows. Knocked from side to side under a brutal assault.

Rage fills me, my blood boiling, I dig deep, calling in the magic of my joined companions.

"Aviella," Killian says, the mage appearing next to me.

He's glowing a brilliant blue, and then next to him is Luca with his aqua-blue piercing eyes, long blonde hair flowing. They weave their hands together, magical energy flowing with each motion they make, forming symbols in the air.

"My dad's in there," I say, pointing down to the ground below us.

"It's a dream, Aviella," Gavin says, appearing out of nowhere. Gavin with his dreadlocks and his easy smile grabs my arm and squeezes.

"No, the shadows have him, I saw them," I argue.

As I say it, red eyes light up around us. Thousands of them, maybe millions. They're everywhere. So many of them, there's no way we can stand against it alone.

"It's a trap," Ronan says, stepping out of a shadow.

His tattoos glow brightly, and he puts his arms out to either side. Energy flows from the symbols the other mages were weaving in the air and into him. He glows brighter and brighter, then it explodes out of him, pushing the dark shadows back.

Horrid, spine-tearing screams assault my ears and instinctively I cover them with my hands, clenching my eyes tight.

Magic crawls across my skin, weaving in and out of my very being. It's their magic, calling mine, intertwining, and I know, as I already suspected, they're part of my cabal.

The sound recedes, and I'm able to open my eyes again. The shadows have retreated, but not far. A dozen yards away they swirl, growing darker by the minute.

"We have to get her out of here," Gavin says.

"Any bright ideas on that?" Ronan asks, shaking his head.

The four mages position themselves around me, facing outward. They each weave magic and in a moment of inspiration, I flow magic to them instead of taking theirs into me.

Gavin glances over his shoulder, smiling and giving me a nod.

It's a moment before things storm out of the shadows, attacking from all sides at once.

They form a shield that domes over all of us, and the things slam against it. There's a sizzle each time they hit, not unlike a bug zapper. Momentarily, I think we're going to be okay, but then I see the sweat forming on each of their brows.

Flowing magic to them as fast as I can, I'm delving into my own reserves as the assault continues without end.

The ground rumbles as a roar echoes off our dome followed by another and another.

"Cavalry's arriving," Killian says.

"About time," Gavin says.

I touch each of them in turn because it's easier to flow magic to them with the physical contact. As they speak, I glance up and see the three dragons' arrival.

It takes my breath away to see them in their native state. Flying with a graceful beauty that is awe-inspiring. They're massive, so big and powerful, I don't know how anything could ever stand against them.

They dive at our dome, and as one they breathe fire, burning away the shadows around us. The fire hits our dome and flows across it. The temperature inside skyrockets and stinging sweat pours into my eyes.

As the flames pass, we're left standing but the ground around is devastated. Tynan, Shen, and Alaric walk towards us with an easy, ambling gait as if nothing is going wrong.

"They have my dad!" I yell.

All seven of the men look at me, but Tynan is the one who moves forward and takes my hands.

"Aviella," he says. "This is a dream. You need to wake up now."

"No," I shake my head. "No, they have him. I know I'm dream walking, but they have him and we have to get him!"

"We will," he says, his eyes holding mine. "Now wake up."

He leans in and kisses my forehead.

I jerk awake in sweat-covered sheets. Thrashing my way clear, I stumble out of bed and look around wild-eyed.

"The mages are here," Efram says from the foot of my bed.

I jump at the sound of his voice, whirling towards him, magic force ready to be let go.

"Efram?" I ask.

"Yes," he says. "You should change. They're waiting on you."

He walks out of my bedroom, leaving me alone with my pounding heart and shortness of breath.

After collapsing onto the edge of the bed, I hold my head in my hands until at last I calm down. Then I dress and prepare to go see the mages. Someone better have some damn answers.

CHAPTER SIXTEEN

AVIELLA

*E*fram leads the way to a lower-level set of rooms. As we pass through the door, my skin tingles and I stop, looking up, down, and around.

"Magic?" I ask.

"Wards," Efram answers. "Surprising you felt them, they're well-made and you're factored into them."

"Factored into?" I ask.

"Included in the spell," he clarifies. "It won't block your entrance."

"Ah," I nod my understanding.

We walk down a hallway barely wide enough for us to be side by side, then turn a corner and go through a door. The room we enter isn't big and looks like it was probably a storage area. Metal shelves line three out of four rooms but the biggest things in the room are the four mages.

"Glad you're here," Killian says.

"Was that real?" I ask, not explaining what I'm asking about. They'll either know it or they won't.

"Unfortunately, yes, mostly," Gavin answers when Killian glances at him.

"They have my dad, we have to move. Now," I say.

"We don't know that," Killian says.

"I do," I answer.

"No, you don't," Luca says. "You know what the Shadow wants you to believe."

"I felt him there!" I yell, my magic buzzing inside of me like an angry hornets' nest. I need a target to let out my frustration on, and he'll do fine.

"You think you did," Gavin moves between Luca and me. "I told you, it's mostly true, not completely. They're trying to manipulate you."

"Aviella," Efram says, putting a hand on my arm and gently pulling me around to face him.

"What?" I snap.

Efram doesn't speak, staring with his kind eyes, and I know I'm being a bitch. The anger deflates like a popped balloon, leaving me deflated and empty.

"I have to save him, damn it," I curse, tears welling.

No one speaks as I collapse into a rickety chair and hold my head in my hands. Breathing deeply, I get myself under control before facing them. Gavin comes over after a couple of minutes and uses his magic to scan over me.

"You're different," he says softly.

"Yeah," I say, straightening and looking at them all. "Sorry. I'm... really frustrated."

"We understand," Luca says, smiling. "It's not easy, we all get that."

As I meet each of their eyes one at a time, Killian's hold me the longest. They smolder with an inferno of desire, and the intertwining connection of our fates throbs with unspent passion. Suddenly the tension in the room shifts to something completely different than my anger.

Each of the men assembled wants me and I want them. Sexual energy pulses between them and me, flowing back and forth and growing stronger. It's so fast and intense I barely suppress a moan.

"The dragons?" Gavin asks, surprise clear in his tone. "How?"

Efram clears his throat, pulling everyone's attention.

"We should get to the matter at hand," Efram says, giving me an out from saying out loud what happened between the dragons and me.

I take it, nodding my agreement.

"Right, why are you here?" I ask the mages. "You don't show up for no reason or to say hi. What's going on?"

"The girl you healed, she's an Innocent," Killian says.

"Right, I wondered why you hadn't gathered her in already," I say.

"Someone here was hiding her from us," Luca says.

"Merrick," I growl, clenching a fist.

What is that witches' game? He's up to something I'm sure, and I don't trust him fully. It could be that he's set himself against the dragons, but I don't think so. There's something more to him that I can't put my finger on. If nothing else, he irritates me.

"What do we know of him?" Gavin asks the group.

"He leads an underground coven of witches," Efram says. "He's not a bad guy. He hates what the dragons have done with the bunker and wants to enact reform, make things better for everyone."

"Better defined by whom?" I ask.

The look on Efram's face makes me regret my words as soon as they leave my mouth. I hurt him, and I certainly didn't mean to. He trusts Merrick, even though I don't know why any more than I know why I don't trust him.

The mages look at each other, and I know they are talking without saying anything out loud. Efram shifts uncomfortably, avoiding my eyes.

"One way or another, if there is one Innocent here who's been hidden, it's likely that there are more," Gavin says, breaking the rising tension.

Suddenly all four mages turn to the door, alert and ready to act. Magic crackles through the room with a hissing sound, making the hair on my arms stand on end. Luca moves to the door, quick as lightning, and I notice his right hand has a soft blue glow around it.

He glances over his shoulder at Gavin, he waits until Gavin nods, and he throws the door open, stepping back into a defensive posture at the same time.

Merrick stands in the doorway with his palms held out and open, an easy grin on his face. All of us look from one to another quickly.

"I invited him," Efram says.

Gavin's face darkens, but it passes, quickly replaced by stoic blankness.

"Come in," Gavin says.

Merrick walks in, looking at each of the mages in turn before his eyes stop on me. He grins as if this is the most natural meeting in the world.

"Surprised to see the Mage's Guild showing up here," Merrick says.

"We go where we're needed," Luca says testily.

"Right," Merrick grins. "Needed by who?"

Luca's hand balls into a fist and he steps towards Merrick, fully prepared to take the first swing, but Killian stops him with a hand on his chest. Merrick stands ready, his own chest puffing out and he preens like a peacock, waiting for the mage to try something.

"Enough," I snap. "We don't have time for your antics, Merrick."

"Right," Gavin says, stepping into the opening I made for

him. "You have an Innocent here, we need to collect her, and any others you have."

"I don't know what you're talking about," Merrick says, but the look on his face makes it clear that he's lying through his teeth.

"Merrick—" Efram starts.

"Clearly there's little time to organize anyway," Merrick says, cutting him off. "You must all know that an evacuation is going to happen. The shadow factions don't send the kind of forces like that to 'test the waters', they intend to seize Aviella. The Dragons will insist on moving her and themselves as well."

"We'll cross that bridge when we come to it," Ronan says.

"We're at it," Merrick says.

"I'll take your word for it," Ronan says, his eyes glowing like dark stones as he locks gazes with the leader of the coven.

"Sure," he says. "You all do that. Good luck finding those, what was it? Innocents? Yeah, best of luck with that."

He walks out of the room with a swagger that pisses me off. As the door closes behind him, I glare at Efram. Efram shrugs and shakes his head.

"I don't know," Efram says. "He's not normally like that."

"We'll have to go around him," Gavin says matter-of-factly.

"What about an evacuation?" Killian asks. "We'll have to move fast if the Dragons are doing that."

Closing my eyes, I focus on my connection to the dragons. They're doing something intently, but I can't pick up what. Opening my eyes again, I look at the men and shake my head.

"They're intent on something," I say. "I'm not sure what."

Efram frowns and looks away from me. The mages look at each other, then as one they nod.

"Okay," Ronan says. "We need to get to it."

"Right, I'll go back upstairs, see if I can get a handle on what Tynan is planning," I say.

"Good," Gavin says, nodding before turning his attention to Ronan and Luca.

"I'll escort you," Efram offers and I smile, accepting his offer.

I'm sure he feels bad about how things went with Merrick. It's not his fault, really, and I don't blame him for Merrick. That doesn't change that I don't understand his trust in the witch. Maybe he'll tell me about it.

"I'll come too," Killian offers suddenly, and I feel Efram's instant disappointment, but he doesn't object.

"Okay," I agree, albeit a little reluctantly.

Killian doesn't seem to pick up on any of that as he bounces over to my left side, opposite Efram, and takes my arm. Efram takes my other side, and we head for the upper floors.

We exchange small talk as we walk, but nothing meaningful. Thankfully it becomes comfortable very quickly. Killian is so easy going and laid back that it's impossible for the tension to remain high with him around.

When we reach the top floor and the guards come into sight, Killian stops. His hand on my arm stops me too.

"Could I have a word?" he asks. "Privately?"

He looks over my head at Efram. Uncertain what's happening, I look for Efram's agreement as well. Efram's jaw tightens, but that's the only sign of disagreement.

"Of course," he says, walking on down the hall to the guards and making small talk as he approaches them.

"Here," Killian says, pulling on my arm and guiding me into an alcove that's out of the line of sight.

It's small, forcing us to be close to each other, and I'm instantly aware of his size and the manliness of him. He has a musky smell with hints of pine to it that is incredibly entic-ing, lighting an instant fire in my core.

He looks down into my eyes, and the mask is gone. He looks fairly sick with passion and the struggle to contain it. The burning in his eyes promises pleasures that I desperately want to enjoy.

"What?" I ask, my voice hoarse and raspy as I force words out of my closed throat.

He doesn't speak for a long moment, staring into my eyes, his hands gripping my arms. He swallows hard, and I watch his Adam's apple move up and down.

"You've grown," he says at last.

"Did you think I wouldn't?" I ask. Impulsively, I touch his cheek, trailing my fingers along the stubble.

"Not so fast," he says, leaning closer.

His breath is warm against my skin and my cheeks burn in response.

"There's no time," I breathe.

"No, there's not," he whispers, his lips grazing mine.

I rise on my toes stretching up to meet his lips, but he pulls back as I do.

"Not like this," he says, an exertion of will I don't think I could muster.

I struggle with my desires and urges, fighting against grabbing his cock, knowing damn well that will throw his cautions to the wind. He's right, this isn't the time or the place. No matter how much my body wants him, but its more than my body. His power calls, and something in my own powers hungers to open that connection.

"Right," I gasp, pushing myself back from his chest. Shaking my head, I say it again, affirming myself. "Right."

"We're going to need your help," he says, at last, biting his lower lip and breathing slowly in and out.

His struggle is so intense I feel it happening against my skin.

"Okay," I say.

"If he won't give us those Innocents, we'll have to go around him," he continues.

"Right," I agree. "Let me know what you need."

I can't stand anymore of this so I step out into the hall, putting distance between our bodies before I do something foolish.

He follows, and for an instant our eyes meet, and all the promises and desires flood through both of us. I feel it reciprocating in him, and I know that he will be an amazing lover, when the time comes.

Not now, Aviella. Not now, but soon.

He smiles, his easy, lazy-looking smile then turns and heads back for the lower floors. I linger, watching him go before turning and going to Efram and my rooms.

CHAPTER SEVENTEEN

EFRAM

I try not to watch her talking to him. I have no claim on her or her attentions, I remind myself. It doesn't stop the stabbing pain in my chest or make my breathing any easier. She's not mine, not fully and completely.

And what right would I have to her? The world needs her. We all need her, she's too special for me alone. I know it beyond a shadow of a doubt. I suspected it not long after I first found her, but now, all we've been through, there isn't a shadow of doubt in my mind.

She's the one.

Our one hope, and if the Shadow gets her, the path this world is going to go down isn't good. No one really understands the Apocalypse. It's not the end of the world, it's a new beginning. The question is what direction will that beginning go? What will the new world be like?

That question revolves around Aviella.

If she wins, defeats the Shadow, the world will be one created by her effort and her vision. If she loses, then the darkness will prevail, and the world will fall to the Shadow at long last.

"Hey," Aviella says, walking up and pulling me from my thoughts.

"Everything okay?" I ask, carefully keeping my voice neutral and not prying.

"Yeah, I think so," she says, staring down the hall at Killian's retreating form. She shakes her head before turning her attention to me. "Let's go to my rooms."

"Lead the way," I say.

The two guards to the upper floor stop us as we walk up.

"Only you," the man on the left says, his hand on my chest.

"Right," Aviella snorts. "He's with me."

"We have our orders. We're on full lock-down," he says, not moving his hand.

Aviella bristles, ducks under his arm so that she is in his face.

"I don't care who gave you what orders. He's. With. Me."

The man's smart enough that his face pales at her heavily implied threat but he shakes his head.

"I'm sorry," he says, barely above a whisper. "Orders. Call it in?"

He says the last to the other guard who has a hand inside his jacket. As if a gun is going to do any good against either of us.

The other man pulls his hand out from his jacket and touches his ear. He mutters unintelligibly while Aviella and his partner stare each other down. No one moves while we wait. The tension is high. I wonder if these two are sensitive to the magic. It's making the air electric, like the building of a massive storm, but only if you're aware of it. I've found that normal humans don't sense magic.

"He's cleared," the other guard says and the tension drops.

The man drops his arm off my chest and steps back to stand by the door again. Aviella glares as she sweeps past him, and I follow in her wake. It's not his fault, he's doing his job. The tension in the Bunker is at an all-time high. I can only imagine the dragons' reaction to the Shadow Forces infiltration.

Aviella storms the hallway. Her magic is a cloud of electric energy filling the space, roiling, looking for a target, any target, to take out her frustration and rage on. I can't stop the smile playing across my face as my chest expands and my heart beats harder. She's perfect. Every bit of her is so beautiful.

I've been around a long time and no woman has ever wormed her way into my heart like her. She's done it all without trying to. I've never known anyone who is filled with such passion for life, for helping others, or in any way better suited to change the world.

She unlocks the door to her suites and I follow her in. We both come to a stop facing the three dragons. Tynan's eyes alight with a fiery passion the moment he lays eyes on Aviella. The sexual tension the dragons exude has always been over the top, yet somehow, they take it to a new level. Their desire hits against me like the waves of the ocean as a storm rolls in. Hard, fast, almost I take a step back, but I'm able to brace myself against it.

"Aviella," Tynan says, his voice silky smooth.

Aviella stiffens the moment he speaks, and instantly the connection I have with her throbs with its own sexual energy. Her desire is every bit as high as theirs. An image flashes through my thoughts of her and the three dragons. An ache in my chest so deep I can't catch a breath hits me. Jealousy, anger, and something more, deeper rises but I can't let myself give in to it. Especially that deeper thought, that bare instant of recognizing my jealousy is in part I want to give her all my attention *with* the dragons. A desire to put her on the pedestal she deserves as the four of us worship her as the goddess she is, treat her as she deserves to be treated.

"What are you guys doing here?" she asks.

The three dragons exchange a look, but don't answer. I step in.

"Tynan," I say. "Rafe and Nathaniel will be back soon. Silas and I can keep Aviella safe, and once they're back, there's nothing the Shadow Forces can throw that we can't hold off."

Shen snorts, a derisive grin on his face. Alaric steps towards me shaking his head.

"You," he says, making the single word into an accusation. "Can stand against the Shadow?"

"I said that we can," I answer, not backing down.

"Oh, I see," Alaric says, looking over his shoulder to Shen. "He said 'we', because that makes all the difference."

"Look, you pompous ass," I growl, hands balling into fists. I've had enough of the dragons' arrogance. "There's more at stake here than any petty games you want to play. We have limited resources, we have to do what it takes to keep her safe, yes. More than that, we have to get our next move going. Obviously, the Shadow Forces have penetrated this bunker."

"Obviously," Shen says. "Your powers of observation are outstanding."

Shen steps up next to Alaric. The two dragons glare, doing their best to intimidate me. I'm not having it. If keeping her safe means I have to beat these two down then that is what I'll do.

"You have a spy in your midst," I growl, moving an inch closer to Alaric so that our chests are barely an inch apart. I'm not backing down.

"Or maybe you're the spy," Alaric growls.

"Boys!" Aviella raises her voice.

"Alaric," Tynan says, not raising his voice, but it cuts through to Alaric, and he takes a step back without another word.

"There's plenty of reason to be tense," Aviella says. "Let's not take that out on each other, okay? You three having a dick-waving contest isn't going to help."

The anger is gone with her words. She's right, I can't let them bait me into this. I must learn to ignore them. It's a game to those two and I know it.

"The necroseer is right," Tynan says. "We need to find the traitor and we need to prepare for what is coming next."

"And what is that?" Aviella asks. "We've been holed up here for weeks and now they've found their way in. Are we going to wait even longer, see if they can get another or even a bigger force inside?"

"No, Aviella," Tynan says. "I only ask for your patience, a little bit more. The time for action is nearly upon us."

She grits her teeth, glaring at Tynan, then nods sharply.

"Fine," she snaps. "A few days, and then we move, with or without you."

"Agreed," Tynan says, without a hint of upset at her tone.

Watching her, a sense of awe fills me. She's commanding not only a dragon, but a Horseman of the Apocalypse. A dragon marked by God. All of that, and the dragon doesn't blink an eye. She's grown from the lost little orphan girl to an incredible woman who commands the men around her. She is our leader. She is the one hope.

She's scared, I feel that along the connection between us, and I see it in her eyes. In the way they flit from one thing to another. The way she jumps at any unexpected sound. In her magic, that is always close and ready to explode. If she wasn't scared though, I'd be worried. It's the only sane response to what we face.

"All right," I say. "Now that we're all in agreement."

"We have things to prepare," Tynan says, his dark eyes locking on me. "I am leaving her in your care, necro-seer."

His words settle on my shoulders with a weight all their own, and magic tingles across my skin. In an instant I recognize what he's done and anger flashes white-hot. He laid a geas, a powerful compulsion, on me. Son of a bitch!

Glaring, I grit my teeth and bite my tongue, saying nothing. I don't want Aviella to know, and she's distracted enough that she missed the magical transfer. Tynan smiles, a half-grin but the delight shining in his eyes says it all.

"Fine," I say through my clenched teeth. "Why don't you all take your leave. I'll make *sure* things are handled here."

"I'm sure you will," Tynan says, smug grin fixed on his face.

It takes all my power to not punch him square in it. Ass.

The dragons take their leave, and finally Aviella and I are alone. She shakes her head, then walks into the small kitchen.

"Tea?" she asks.

"Please," I answer, going to stand next to her and offering to help.

We make two steaming cups, then take seats in her living space. Silence reigns as we sit and I watch her, waiting for what, I don't know. She sits with her feet pulled up under her, two hands on the cup that she blows on, then sips.

"He's an ass," she says at last.

"He?" I ask, feigning I don't know she means Tynan.

"Tynan," she answers. "An ass, but damn good in a fight."

"Yes, he is," I agree.

"Do you really think they'll be back soon?" she asks.

"I do," I say, understanding she's asking about Rafe and Nathaniel.

"Good," she says. "I'm sick of waiting."

"I understand," I say.

She falls silent, contemplating something while staring into her tea cup. When she looks up, the shy, lonely orphan girl shines in her eyes.

"Efram…" she starts, then stops. She inhales deeply, shakes her head, then bites her lip. I wait, patient. "Do you love me?"

My heart stops. I can't breathe. My guts clench tight, my throat closes, time slows to a crawl. She stares, waiting, and in that instant time speeds up. My heartrate gallops and I gasp a deep breath.

"Yes," I exhale. "With all my heart."

A smile shifts across her face, and she's radiant. A brilliant sun and I want to burn in her fire.

"Thank you," she says, softly. "You're first. The one I trust fully."

She yawns, rolls her neck around, then shakes her head. I don't have any words to respond so I sit silently and watch. This is so far beyond desire. We're in uncharted waters, no lighthouse in sight, no buoys, no guideposts to tell me where to go next.

"I'm wiped," she says. "You mind if I sleep?"

"Of course not," I say, rising to my feet.

I take her hand and lead her to her bedroom. She turns to me, and rising onto her toes, she kisses me with a soft, burning passion. Embracing her, I return the kiss, but fully intend to go no further. It's not the time yet, but I know our time will come.

She breaks the kiss, one hand resting on my chest as she drops back flat on her feet.

"Good night," she says.

"Good night," I say, stepping out and closing the door behind me.

CHAPTER EIGHTEEN

AVIELLA

*O*n my bed, I curl up on my side, pulling the pillow tight under my head. My thoughts spin in a frenzy along with an overwhelm of emotions. Efram is standing guard outside my door. I'm aware of his presence, and it's comforting.

I think, maybe, if I'd asked, he'd be in here with me. Thing with him is though, I'm not sure. He's stoic, strong, and unwilling to give in to the desire I know he feels for me. Although, none of that matters, really, because I know he loves me.

When he said the words, the weight of them carried the truth. He reciprocates my feelings for him as strongly as mine. That is enough, for now. When I yawn, I realize how tired I am. So damn tired. As sleep creeps over me my last thoughts are of Rafe and Nathaniel. Damn, I miss them. I wonder if I could reach one of them on the dreamscape. Find out where they are?

∽

When I open my eyes, I look around with a strange sense of *déjà vu*. The gray fog of the dreamscape surrounds me, but it's not dark or menacing as it has been in the past. Apparently free of the Shadow taint, for the moment at least.

Smiling, I think about Rafe, his snarky attitude would be a perfect relief to my tension. As I do the fog darkens, and I know he's in the under realms. That's not an area I can go to without putting myself into massive danger.

Fine, I'll look for Nathaniel.

When I shift my thoughts to the angel, a warm glow forms in my core, radiating out through my limbs. His presence is a golden light, and I have a sense of the direction, so I think myself into motion towards him.

The fog grows lighter, fading from a dirty gray to a soft gray, and then it changes to white. As it shifts, a new connection opens to something… more. I stop and look into myself, trying to understand what is happening. I've never felt anything like it.

Power. Absolute, overwhelming, but it has a quality that I can't quantify. Love, but that word doesn't encompass it. It's too small a word to contain the breadth and depth of this. Nathaniel is close. His wings wrap around me, mystically at least, because he's not here physically.

Images flash through my thoughts, a message, but it doesn't make sense. I can't comprehend what I'm seeing. A fork in a path, and I'm standing at it, looking down each one. No, it's more than that, and it's less.

Waves of dizziness rush over me, and I collapse to the ground. The blindingly white mist flows up my arms. A small part of me is afraid, but I know there's nothing to fear. As it rises towards my head, it brings comfort, a sense of belonging, and that unfathomable depth of caring.

When I look up, a figure stands before me that is only an

outline of blinding white light. A hand reaches out of the light and touches my cheek.

～

I'M SITTING UP, I'M GASPING, I'M LOOKING AROUND THE ROOM wildly, I'm trying to orient myself once more. I haven't been asleep long. I hear Efram shifting in the chair beyond my door. Shaking my head, I lie down and fall into a deep sleep.

In the morning, I wake up and go to make some coffee. Efram is awake when I emerge, eyes heavy with dark circles, but he smiles when I walk out.

"Sleep good?" he asks.

"Yeah," I say.

I know I was going to tell him something when I woke up, something about a dream? I can't recall what it was. Stretching my arms over my head, I pop my back. It actually feels like I had lots of sleep last night. I'm well rested and ready to go for the day.

"I've made coffee," Efram says, motioning to the kitchen area. "And there are some pancakes if you want them."

"Hmm, pancakes!" I say, then go and pour myself a cup of coffee.

"I need to go for a bit," he says, rising.

"Why?" I ask, unable to keep the disappointment out of my voice.

He moves over to the dining bar that separates the kitchen area from the sitting space and leans on it heavily. Instantly I feel bad for him. He's exhausted, beyond exhausted.

"You should sleep," I say, putting a hand on his arm.

He snorts and shakes his head. "No rest for the wicked."

"You're far from wicked," I observe.

"I'm no angel either," he says. "I'll leave that gig to Nate."

We laugh at his joke then our eyes meet, and a fresh tension settles on us. The push-pull of our relationship, my desire for him, and his resistance to giving in to his desire makes it difficult. Our connection is strong already, and I know that if we join further, that will only increase. I'm not going to push him, though. I care too much for him to do that.

"Guess I'll hang out here," I say at last.

"Safest," he agrees. "I'll be back before long. I want to talk to Merrick, see if I can convince him he needs to give those Innocents to the Mages guild."

I bristle at the mention of Merrick, but don't say anything. Trying to cover over my no answer, I sip my coffee. Efram watches me, and it's clear he knows what I'm thinking. There's nothing more to say about it anyway.

"Be safe, Efram," I say.

Longing hits me deep and hard. I grip his arm tight. I don't want him to go. I want him at my side, always. He's my rock through the storm that is my life. He stares at my hand on his arm. This is it! He's going to give, finally! He covers my hand with his, and my heart races, my mouth goes dry, and my lower bits grow wet.

The moment stretches. Yes. Please, I need this…

He takes his hand off of mine, smiles, then meets my eyes.

"I'll be back soon," he says. "Nothing to worry about."

Disappointment is a bitter pill. I watch him leave, all worked up with no relief in sight. Damn it. Tynan flitters through my thoughts, but the instant he does, I sense he's focused on something intently. He's not going to come and offer any relief.

Ugh.

I eat the pancakes and finish the pot of coffee, trying to take my mind off the pulsing ache in my lady parts. Damn it Efram, you're the only one who leaves me like this. When I finish eating, I wash off the dishes then look around my empty rooms.

Alone. Again. Waiting. Again. This sucks so much.

I plop down on the loveseat, grab the book resting on the table, and turn to where I left off. Maybe I can lose myself in the story and pass the time. My thoughts are in so much turmoil that the words on the page barely form a picture for me. Obstinately I keep reading.

An hour passes, and then there's a knock at the door. It's too early for Efram to have returned, so I have no clue who is there. I walk over and answer.

"Hello," Killian says, smiling broadly.

Ronan is next to him, but his attention is on the hallway and looking around.

"Hey," I say, surprised they made it past the floor guards. "What's up?"

"Can we talk?" he asks, nodding his head towards my room.

"Sure," I say, stepping to one side.

He walks in, his body brushing against mine as he passes, and my skin fevers at that slightest touch. The barely repressed desire Efram left me with races to the fore of my thoughts. Ronan turns his back and takes up a guard position, so I shut the door, leaving him outside.

Swallowing hard, I try to get myself under control before I turn to Killian. My heart is pounding in my throat, so I swallow hard, forcing it back down and moisture back into my mouth.

"How's Rowan?" I ask, filling the space between us with something innocuous and safe.

"She's great," he says. "She sends her love."

"Good, send mine back, please?" I ask, he nods then his face turns serious.

"We're preparing to go around Merrick," he says. "We know they're going to attack again soon, so time is short."

"Right," I agree. I motion towards the chairs, and he takes one. I sit down opposite him, waiting for him to say the real reason for his visit.

His eyes smolder with the promises of pleasures that I desperately want. Efram left me worked up and now I want relief. The way Killian looks at me, his magic caressing mine, intertwining, all tell me he feels the same. He swallows before continuing to speak, and I can't help but notice the rise in his pants.

"We wanted to check on you," he says. "Before we leave again."

"We?" I ask, arching an eyebrow.

He hesitates, eyes burning hotter, bulge growing bigger.

"I," he corrects himself. "I wanted to."

The tension in the air is thick. He leans towards me and I towards him, pulled to each other by the gravity of our mutual desires. Standing, he closes with me, leaning, and I lean back into the cushions. His body hovers over me, almost touching. The intensity of his presence is intoxicating. His lips are close to mine but not touching. His breath warms my skin as he hovers.

"There's no time," he whispers.

"Make it," I answer, touching his arms then tracing my fingers up them and clasping my hands behind his neck.

The world rocks, and not in a metaphysical, sexual way. Killian is thrown to one side, and I'm bounced off the chair, landing hard on my ass.

A trumpeting roar follows the violent shaking of the ground. There's a pounding on the door, but I'm disoriented, the fast switch from almost sex to this is too much. Touching the floor with both hands, I ground myself and push off, getting back on my feet.

"What in the…" I say.

The pounding on the door grows louder, more insistent. Killian grabs my shoulders, making sure I'm steady on my feet. Ronan appears inside the door but it hasn't opened. He's see-through, like a hologram.

"Shadow-forces, it's an attack!" he yells looking over at us.

"Shit," Killian says. He looks from me to Ronan.

"We have to get the Innocents out of here, now," Ronan says.

"What about Aviella?" Killian asks, crossing to the door and throwing it open to let Ronan walk in.

The image disappears as the real thing walks in.

"She's not the priority, she has to stay in play," Ronan grimaces.

"I'm not leaving her," Killian says. "She's alone, and none of the other Chosen are here with her."

The Chosen? That's new. Ronan looks conflicted, his eyes going from me to the hall behind him.

"There are guards," he says, uncertainty in his voice.

"It's not enough!" Killian says. "I'll stay, you go help."

"We're going to need you," Ronan says.

Another roar echoes through the open door and the walls shake. The book I'd left lying next to the chair falls to the ground with a clatter, causing all of us to jerk in that that direction.

"Let me through!" Efram's voice from the hall.

Pushing past Killian and Ronan, I go out the door. At the end of the hallway the two guards are trying to hold Efram back. I step out in time to see him hit one of them in the jaw while ducking the arm of the other.

He steps past them running towards me. Something screeches somewhere in the bunker, the sound of it echoing off the walls. Efram races up to me, grabs my arms, staring at me wide-eyed.

"Are you okay?" he asks.

"I'm fine," I smile.

Killian and Ronan step out into the hall, and Efram looks at them, then me in quick succession. I clearly see the thoughts running across his face. He thinks I've slept with them too, which I haven't, yet. He's going to have to come to terms with this new life we're living, but I'm not going to push. I'm certain he will, in his own time and way.

"They attacked Tynan," Efram says, letting go of my arms and stepping back.

"Directly?" Killian asks.

"Yes," Efram says. "It was an ambush. It's been stopped, but it was big and not a feint. They really tried to take him out."

We all look at each other, letting the implications of that sink in.

"Their marks," I say, not meaning to speak out loud, but I know I did when all three of the men before me turn my way.

"What about them?" Efram asks.

I meet each of their eyes, deciding how much I should say, but these are my men. My most trusted companions. If I can't trust them, then who can I trust?

"The dragons, they're no longer marked," I say. "That's why the Shadow wants them off the board. I'm certain of it."

"No longer marked? You're kidding, how?" Ronan ask. "How do you know this?"

Efram looks away, his cheeks coloring and his hands balling into fists. An ache stabs into my chest.

"Because I did it," I plow forward, knowing that my words hurt Efram, but this isn't the time to hold back.

Killian and Ronan look at each other but don't say anything.

"Right, this will move up the time table," Efram says, changing the subject.

"We have to move the Innocents now," Killian says. "No time to delay."

"Yeah," Ronan says, his eyes lingering on me with a longing gaze. He grits his teeth, then nods.

"I'll stay with Aviella," Efram says. "I tried talking to Merrick, but he's not budging. He's certain he's doing the right thing and protecting them, but there's no way he's going to cooperate."

"Then we'll do this the hard way," Killian says, cracking his knuckles and rolling his shoulders.

"Keep in mind, he's a good man," Efram says. "He's doing what he thinks is best."

"Sure," Ronan says. "We'll be in and out before he knows they're gone."

The two mages race out the door and I'm left alone with Efram.

CHAPTER NINETEEN

RONAN

*W*alking away from her is the hardest thing I've ever had to do.

I know damn well she's in danger. They may have targeted Tynan with this attack, but they're only trying to take him to get to her.

"Tynan is going to move her," I say.

"Of that there is no doubt," Killian says.

"What happened in there?" I ask. Killian doesn't answer as we run through the halls side by side. "Killian?"

He glances at me before focusing his eyes forward.

"Nothing," he says, terse.

"You don't feel like 'nothing' happened," I observe, keeping pace when he increases his speed, obviously trying to avoid my line of questions.

"You know our fates as well as I do," he says.

"Yeah," I agree. "Did you?"

"No," he snaps. "Close, but no."

I fall silent, letting my thoughts wander. No matter how much I want to turn around and go back to her, I can't. I've sworn an Oath, and no matter how heavy it lies on me, I have to follow it. There is no choice.

"She's special," I say, not particularly expecting a response.

"Yes," Killian agrees.

People are thronging the halls ahead, milling about in confusion. We fight our way through the crowd, trying not to use magic to do so, but frustration takes over. A quick look and nod from Killian, then we both channel magic. The crowd parts like the Red Sea, and we run through while they struggle to comprehend. It closes behind us the moment we pass through, not giving them time to analyze their actions.

Aviella is still dominating my thoughts. When I swore my Oath to the Order, so many ages ago, I thought I'd lived life. I'd known women, fallen in and out of love, and I knew I needed to have a higher purpose. The Order was that purpose and calling. I've been happy serving my role in it since.

Until her. She changes everything.

How can one woman have such a hold on me? She's beautiful, that goes without saying, but I've known thousands of pretty women. That alone would never turn my head. No, Aviella is special. It reverberates through everything about her. In her magic, her looks, her soul shines out and of all the Innocents we've sheltered, she stands above them. Her heart is more than pure, it's perfect.

"Do we know what Tynan is planning?" I ask, feeling a sense of despair that is foreign to me. The idea of not being near her becomes harder and harder.

"Not yet," Killian says, shaking his head. "The dragon is cunning, and he has his brothers with him as well as Silas."

"Right, I mean we can find them, but if we know where he's planning on going, maybe we can scout ahead. Get the lay of the land?" I ask.

"Gavin isn't going to go for that," he says.

"Right," I say. "Ours is to protect, not to intervene before it's time," I say, imitating Gavin's voice.

"Exactly," Killian laughs.

"If we don't intervene soon, there's not going to be a planet left to intervene in," I say.

"It won't get that far," Killian says confidently.

"We can't let it," I say.

"First step is to bypass Merrick. We asked nicely and he didn't listen, so let's get in and get what we came for," Killian says. "Being busy is the best way to keep your mind off of her."

I almost stumble in shock when he says that. He hasn't read my thoughts—I'd know it. When I look at him, I know how he knew. He's feeling the same pull as I am.

"Right," I agree, focusing my attention on getting to the others so we can take Merrick out of the equation.

CHAPTER TWENTY

AVIELLA

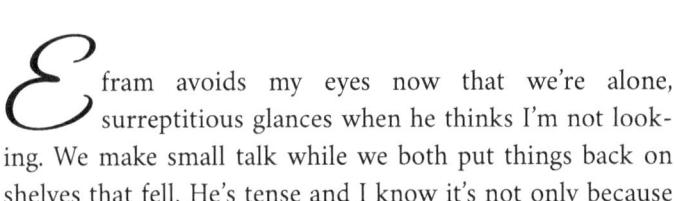

*E*fram avoids my eyes now that we're alone, surreptitious glances when he thinks I'm not looking. We make small talk while we both put things back on shelves that fell. He's tense and I know it's not only because of the attack. It continues until at last I've had enough.

"What?" I ask, hand on hip, daring him to say nothing with my glare.

He's putting a book on a shelf and stops the moment I speak but doesn't turn to face me. He holds stock still and silent. I wait him out, two can play this game.

"Nothing," he says when he finally speaks.

"Efram," I say. "Don't lie to me. Not you, not ever."

His jaw tightens but he turns. Our eyes lock, the tension increases, then it drops away and he nods.

"Yeah," he agrees. "You're right."

"Of course I am," I give him a smile to ease the sting.

"Aviella," he says, stopping, his eyes drop from mine, and he looks around the room sighing heavily. Patient, I wait. He has to work this out for himself. "It's hard. I have no right, but that doesn't make my role in this easier."

"Your role?" I ask.

His eyes glance up, then dart away again. His brow furrows.

"Yes, my… role," he says, obviously choosing the word carefully.

Closing the space between us, I put my hands on his arms. Warmth emanates from the point of contact.

"Hey," I say, moving my head to meet his far-off gaze. "Talk to me, please."

"This," he says, raising his hands and motioning between us. "Us, them, all of us. It's not something I ever thought of. I don't know how to… be in this situation."

"I get it," I say, placing the tips of my fingers on his jaw. "I do. Take your time, Efram. It's fine. I never, well, expected this either, you know?"

A smile flits across his face.

"You deserve it," he says, barely a whisper. "You deserve everything."

"No," I shake my head. "I'm not worth all this, really. I don't know how this all came to be, I didn't do anything to earn it. Maybe it's fate. Maybe it's the hand of God. I don't know, all I know is that it's more than that it feels right. It's the end game. I need each of you. I care about each of you, deeply. You, Efram, you. I love you."

His eyes jerk to mine, and his mouth opens. He starts to speak, but then he changes the action, grabbing me and lifting me off my feet.

Our lips meet and it's electric. All the romance novels I've ever read that talk about the first kiss, their descriptions pale in comparison to his lips on mine. It's not only passion, but a connection. Pathways open between us and energy crackles between us.

Desire, yes, absolutely, but the rest I can't process into words. It's right. He's my rock and the one my soul calls.

When he pulls back for air, I'm breathless. Fire burns in his eyes, and I want it to consume me. I want him to take me, but the next move is his to make, not mine. His passion and his love for me shines in his eyes and on his face, a beacon that will always call me home.

Slowly he lowers me to my feet, his hands cupping my face. He kisses me again, softly, lovingly. Our foreheads rest together, my fingers on the tight muscles of his chest.

"I love you," he says.

"I love you, too," I say.

His hands move back, tangling in my hair, and he tugs my head back, tilting it for another kiss.

Someone pounds on the door so hard they must be trying to break it down.

"What!" I yell, startled and frustrated that this all-important moment is being interrupted.

I storm to the door and throw it open, ready to blast whoever or whatever is on the other side. Silas stands there, but the thing that stops me is Nate. The angel has an arm around Silas, his clothes are torn and dirty, his face is haggard, and he looks at me with haunted eyes.

"Shit," I exhale. "Come in!"

Silas helps Nathaniel through the door which I close. Efram rushes over and takes Nate's other side, helping him to a chair. While the men settle him, I get some water to bring to him. The angel takes it, giving me a grateful smile, and then he takes a long drink.

Silas, Efram, and I look at each other. I'm unsure what to do. Nathaniel leans back in the chair, sets the water on the table, then looks up and gives a wan smile.

"Hello," he says.

"What happened?" I ask.

The angel shakes his head. "It's a bit rough out there."

"I can see that," I say.

"We don't have long," Silas says. "Tynan asks that we all meet."

"When," Efram asks.

"Fifteen minutes," Silas says. "He's even invited the witches."

"You're kidding!" I exclaim. "The mages are planning to go around Merrick and take the Innocents he's hiding."

"When?" Silas and Nathaniel ask at the same time.

Nathaniel rises to his feet, wavers for an instant, then steadies himself. Glancing at Efram, I try to figure out how long it's been.

"Maybe twenty minutes since Killian and Ronan left to meet with the others," Efram answers.

"We have to stop that, there's no time for internal squabbles," Nathaniel says.

There's a weight to his words. The angel has learned something in his travels, but there's no time to hear it. Taking the lead, I race out the door and the others follow in my wake.

"Radio Tynan that the mages are moving on Merrick," I order the guards at the end of my hall.

The biggest of them looks at me blankly but the other touches his ear and is talking rapid-fire. Rolling my eyes at the big, burly man who's been a constant hassle, I resume running down the halls.

Debris litters the main halls. Broken doors, chunks of stone and plaster, pock marks in the floor and walls all point to the battles that took place with the latest Shadow invasion. Fortunately, I don't see any bodies but I'm sure that doesn't mean there were no casualties. The monsters revel in their death tolls.

As we go lower into the Bunker we come across milling crowds. They're lost, scared, and most of them seem to be in shock. They barely respond as we push our way past them. A young, gaunt girl grabs my arm as I pass, her eyes wide, mouth open, tears streaming down her face.

"What do we do?" she cries.

Pausing, I place my hand over hers. Unexpectedly, a warm pulse of energy flows out of me into her. Her eyes widen and clear, her mouth closes.

"Prepare to leave," I tell her. "Help everyone you can."

"Yes," she nods, her face all but glowing with renewed purpose. "Yes!"

She turns and grabs the next person closest to her.

"Pack, pack light, only the most essential things. We have to get ready to move," the girl insists.

I don't stay to watch what happens next because I don't have time. Right now we have to stop the mages from going to war with the witches.

"My life," I comment as we run.

"Huh?" Efram asks.

"We're running to stop a war between mages and witches," I say. "I hang out with dragons, an angel, a demon, a methuselah, and a necroseer. This is my life. Doesn't it all sound more than a bit crazy?"

Efram laughs and Silas does too.

"When you put it that way," Efram says. "Yeah."

We continue our mad dash for the lower floors. As we move closer a tingle rushes over my skin causing the hair on my arms to stand on end.

"Magic," Silas observes.

"You think?" I ask, shaking my head.

"We might be too late," Nathaniel intones, his voice serious as always.

"We can't be," I say.

Still we run faster. A stitch in my side almost causes me to stop but necessity keeps me going through the pain. When we turn the final corner, I'm panting and wishing I'd spent more of my down time doing cardio.

"First rule of the zombie apocalypse," I pant.

"Cardio," Nathaniel says, and all of us look at him.

"I am not out of touch with pop culture," he answers our astonished looks.

"The things I never knew," I say.

"This stops now!" Tynan's voice booms, echoing off the walls and coming back at us in reverb.

The magic that had been filling the air like static electricity on crack suddenly dies, as if it wasn't there at all. It doesn't fade away, it's gone, instantly. It's crazy. I've never felt anything like it.

When we turn the corner, there are the four mages standing in a semi-circle, facing off against Merrick and four of his witches. In between the two groups stands Tynan, looking imperious. A red glowing halo surrounds him as he exerts his dragon nature.

He may have drained the magic or whatever, but they were about to throw at each other but it didn't do anything to stop them beating each other senseless. Merrick has that same self-satisfied grin on his face he usually does that makes me want to slap him. The four of us stop behind the mages.

Merrick's smirk falters for an instant upon seeing us, but he puts it firmly in place and crosses his arms over his chest.

"Cavalry's arrived," he says.

Gavin glances over his shoulder but Tynan looks and smiles. If the devil was made incarnate, he'd probably be Tynan. The delight in his eyes, the sexual, dominating energy he puts out is beyond alpha male. It's a league of its own.

"Aviella," he says my name as if it's an invocation of desire.

His voice caresses my skin, and for a moment there are

only the two of us as his eyes undress me. Efram clears his throat, loudly, breaking in and stopping the fantasy.

"Tynan," I say, swallowing hard to get my heart back down into my chest where it belongs.

The four mages stand down, lowering their arms and unclenching their fists. Merrick's men with him stand down, or as close to it as I think they get. I need to ask Silas or Efram what the difference is between the mages and the witches. I'm sure not going to ask one of the mages. I'm certain it's a touchy subject with them, especially right now.

"You should be upstairs, in your rooms," Tynan says, conversing with me as if there wasn't a brawl about to happen as I arrived.

"Had a feeling I was needed here," I answer, moving past the mages to stand in the middle with Tynan.

"Ah, this is well under control," Tynan says.

"Look, Merrick," Gavin says stepping forward. "We want the Innocents you're protecting. They need to come to Sanctuary with us."

"Trust you? Impossible," Merrick snarls.

"It's the entire purpose of our Order," Gavin bristles. "Our sworn duty."

"Right," one of the witches behind Merrick snorts.

"Your sworn duty," Merrick says. "Making young witches, naturally talented magic users disappear."

"We don't make them disappear!" Luca shouts, stepping forward, fists coming up.

"Your actions say as much," Merrick grins at the reaction —it's exactly what he wants.

"Enough," Tynan says. He doesn't raise his voice or make any threatening moves, but both sides stand down again. If it's out of respect or fear, I'm not sure. "We are civilized beings. Let us discuss this situation as such."

"I'm not sitting down with a shadow-marked dragon," Merrick shakes his head.

"He's not," I say.

"What?" Merrick snaps, turning his attention to me.

"He's. Not," I repeat, emphasizing each word and trying, but failing, to keep my contempt for the witch for bleeding through.

"How can you…" Merrick starts, but he's staring at Tynan and trails off. "Son of a bitch."

Tynan faces him fully and gives him a condescending smile.

"You were saying, Merrick?" Tynan asks.

"That can't be," Merrick says. "It's impossible."

"You keep using that word. I do not think it means what you think it means," Nathaniel intones, and once again I look at the angel with new eyes.

He shrugs, a momentary grin flashing. Silas shakes his head and Efram rolls his eyes. Merrick shakes his head again then frowning he nods his assent.

"Fine," he says. "This way."

He turns and leads the way further down the tunnels, then motions that we should all enter a side room. There is a series of makeshift tables set together creating a long row. We all take seats on the mismatched rickety stools around it.

"Very good," Tynan says, having positioned himself at the head of the tables. "Now. The mages have a job, a duty if you will. I understand you have objections."

"Damn straight I do," Merrick says.

Gavin bristles at his tone, leaning forward, but stops himself speaking when Tynan shoots a glance at him.

"It would be best if you let them take the ones they want," Tynan says. "We are preparing to evacuate the Bunker. Our defenses have been breached and cannot be trusted."

"Shen and Alaric's favorites opened the wards," Nathaniel says.

"What?" Tynan's voice is low and dangerous.

No one speaks, we're all staring at Nate waiting for him to say more. "I tried to get here to stop it, but I was too late. You'll find they are gone."

"Wow, how you like that turn of events?" Merrick snarks.

"Merrick," I say softly. "Snark off one more time, and it will be your last."

Magic crackles around me, reinforcing my words, buzzing inside of me like an angry hornets' nest. I've had enough of his attitude, and I'm going to shut it down. He rises from his seat, but I slam him down with a thought, magic pushing, then holding.

His eyes widen, and for the first time I see him afraid. It washes over me, and some dark part inside of me revels in it. It's glorious knowing this all-powerful witch fears me. Smiling, I consider crushing him and ending it.

Get a grip Aviella! I yell at myself in my head.

That wasn't me, it's a part of the nature I'm picking up from my protectors. Alaric, Shen, Tynan, but also Silas, and even Efram to a degree. They've all got darkness in them. It's part and parcel of who they are, and as I join with them, I take on that as well.

Keeping it under control isn't easy, but I must. I've already struggled with losing myself to Tynan's urges, and if I can't do it, then I have an absolute certainty we'll lose everything. The world literally depends on me keeping my shit in a pile.

Or I'm a delusional megalomaniac. Jury is still out. One way or another, I release Merrick. The moment I do, it's as if everyone at the table takes a breath at once. Merrick gasps aloud, shakes his head, opens his mouth, then snaps it shut.

"Fine," he says, placing his hands on the table.

"I'll have to investigate this," Tynan says. "It doesn't change the matter to hand."

"Above all, it isn't safe here," Ronan says. "We must get the Innocents out of here, and to the safety of Sanctuary."

Merrick's face darkens, but he doesn't speak. Everyone at the table waits with bated breath to see how he will respond. This all comes down to him.

"Fine," he says, sharply.

Blinking, I stare at him in surprise. I didn't expect him to agree.

"Fine?" Tynan asks.

"Yes, fine," he says. "On one condition."

There it is, I knew there had to be more to this than what he was presenting.

"Which is?" Gavin asks.

"My coven has a place in the escape plan," he glares at Tynan while speaking. "We don't get left behind."

Tynan frowns, the only outward sign he gives. Slowly he drums his fingers on the wooden table, never taking his eyes from Merrick. Once more it all hinges on a single decision. Internally, across the connection I have with him, there is turmoil in Tynan. He's debating something intently. Silently I urge him to agree.

"Agreed," Tynan says, turning his gaze from Merrick to me.

"Good," Merrick nods, then rises. "I have work to do then."

"We need them, now," Luca says, rising to his feet with the other mages.

"Sure, go get them," he says to one the witches with him.

The man nods and walks off, apparently in no hurry of his own.

"Thank you," Gavin says.

"It's a trade, nothing more," Merrick says. "Besides I don't have the majority of those who've survived. You've all missed the treasure trove of your so-called 'innocents'."

"What do you mean?" Killian asks.

"The Mega-Church Bunker," Merrick grins evilly. "They've got dozens of them locked up in there."

"How do you know this?" Luca snarls moving to go around the table to Merrick but Killian stops him with a hand on his shoulder.

"Sources," Merrick says, still grinning. "What, you don't have your own?"

"If you know something, spill it, witch," Tynan orders.

"I know what I've said, dragon," Merrick says. "I'll not say more. You may be free of the shadow's mark, but the last of your brood isn't. This may be an alliance, but it's one of necessity, not love."

"You will regret those words," Killian says and this time it's Luca who holds him back.

"Enough," I say, shaking my head. I'm sick of Merrick's games. He's a viper in our midst. "Go, Merrick, before you get hurt."

He opens his mouth to retort, then snaps it shut. Smart man. He nods and leaves without another word. The remaining men turn their attention to me. Warmth floods through my body the moment they have their attention on me, and tingles run across my skin and down into my core.

"I don't trust him," Silas says.

"I know, no one here does," I say, looking at Efram because of all those assembled, he's the only one I'm not sure feels the same. Efram nods his agreement, and I accept it. "End of the day, he's not evil. I don't feel the mark of the shadow on him. He's self-centered and opportunistic, yes, but we know what we're dealing with in that."

"We have to get into the Mega-church bunker," Gavin

says, anger seething around him. "Somehow they've been hiding the Innocents from us."

The four mages exchange a troubled look.

"Right," I say. "Well, I guess we know where we need to go next."

"I have matters to attend to," Tynan says.

"We're going to collect those we're here for," Gavin says. "Will you be okay?"

It takes a moment for it to register that he's talking to me. "Huh? Oh, yeah."

"I'll take care of her," Efram says.

Efram gives Tynan a strange look, but before I can say anything, Silas speaks.

"What's the exit strategy then?" Silas asks.

"We're preparing transport," Tynan says.

"I'll give what aid I can," Silas offers.

"Good," Tynan says, nodding.

Tynan reaches out and grabs me, pulling me tight against him, and kisses me forcefully. Desire rages in him and my own desire responds. I grab his hair, jerk his head back, and now I'm kissing him, taking control for myself.

I break the kiss, pushing him back. He smiles, one hand rising to and touching his lips. He nods thoughtfully and leaves.

"Let's get out of here," I say, ignoring the flabbergasted looks on everyone's faces.

They can think what they want, I'm tired of waiting around, and I'm taking control. I know what has to happen, and we're running out of time. Efram recovers first, taking my hand and together he and I walk out. I do, consciously, put an extra bit of sway into my hips enjoying the sensation of their eyes boring into my back as I leave.

That's right. You're all mine, sooner or later. I grin at the thought then can't stop myself from chuckling.

"Pleased with yourself?" Efram asks.

"Yes," I agree. "Yes I am."

"You did good back there," he says, admiration shining in his eyes. "You're coming into your own."

"Thank you," I say, my chest swelling with pride and emotion.

We make our way through the chaos of the halls of the bunker and up to my rooms, walking hand in hand. Everything is going to hell in a handbasket, but still, I'm certain we'll figure it out. Somehow.

CHAPTER TWENTY-ONE

AVIELLA

*T*he bunker is in full-on panic. Fear pervades so thickly it's in the air. I set about doing what I can to help people get ready to move, with the help of Efram.

Pausing to wipe sweat from my forehead, I look out across the thronging masses and sigh heavily. No matter how much we've accomplished, there is more to do. Tynan and the dragons have outfitted two trains. Amazingly, unlike the human-powered ones I grew up with, these are fueled by coal or wood.

Stocking them with enough supplies to survive the trip outside is proving more time-consuming than I can believe. It's made slower because half the population of the bunker are sick or injured. In the last two attacks by Shadow forces, the regular populace took the brunt of it.

"How much longer?" I ask Efram.

He looks back after he shoves the box he's carrying into an overhead storage bin. "A day, maybe two."

"Can we fit all these people on here?" I ask, looking out the door of the rail car across the mobs of humanity milling about.

Efram places an arm around my waist, holding me loose but close.

"No," he says softly. "If they figure that out though, there will be a riot. Keep it quiet."

I bite my lip. "We can't leave them behind."

"We don't have a choice," he answers.

"Have you seen Nate?" I ask.

"He's busy healing in the sick bay," he says.

"Does he seem… distant to you?" I ask.

Efram pauses, again taking time to look at me.

"Distant how? It's Nate, he's always stand-offish," he says.

"More?" I shrug. "I don't know, feels like he's avoiding me since he got back."

"He'll work it out," Efram assures me.

"I hope so," I say. "I miss him. Besides, who knew he was hip to pop culture."

"The angel has layers," Efram jokes.

"Like an onion," I say in my best bad Shrek impression.

I'd loved those movies when I was little. That was before the Apocalypse hit, before I lost my Dad, before all of this. Sighing, I get back to work and we make progress. The train car we're filling ends up loaded to capacity with food stores and other necessary supplies.

When we call it done, I splash some water on my face at a small basin to rinse off the sweat and dirt. My stomach grumbles loudly, but my mind is on Nate more than eating.

"Want to get dinner?" Efram asks.

"I'm going to find Nate," I say.

Efram does a good job of hiding his grimace, but I still catch it before he can. First I touch his arm, then I squeeze it tightly, then pull him closer to me. When I've pressed myself against him, I wrap my arms around his neck, rise onto my toes, and kiss him.

He stiffens, but only for a moment before relaxing into

the kiss. He returns it, and the passion between us rises. It's not the time, and certainly not the place for more, no matter how much I want to, so I keep it to a kiss. A passionate, deeply intimate kiss, but still only a kiss.

"Be careful," he says, instinctively or consciously knowing I need to confront the angel on my own.

Smiling at him, I touch his sweet, dear face. I let my fingers linger on his jaw as we gaze into each other's eyes. He smiles, turning into my touch and kissing the palm of my hand.

"I will," I answer.

We part ways with that final touch, but the warmth of his skin persists on my fingers. I close that hand to keep his skin's heat as I make my way through the crowds towards the sick bay area. The closer I get, the worse the people look and smell. The odor of death on the air is strong, and it causes a revulsion in me both physical and mystical.

Cots dot the floor with sick people lying on them. They cough and shiver but these are the least bad cases, I know from experience. Nathaniel will be further in, with the seriously ill and injured. Screams fill the air. Pain and suffering are a heavy cloud that I walk through, doing my best to ignore it.

After passing through hanging sheets of plastic, I spot Nathaniel kneeling next to a cot at the back of the room. There are dozens of people lying on them between him and me, caretakers making their way among them. A table sits at the back, covered in blood, and two men in outfits that were once white but are now covered in blood and gore stand behind it. One of them motions, and two other men go and pick up a person, cot and all, and place him on the table.

"No, no, no," the man on the cot protests. "Don't take it, please, god don't take it."

"I'm sorry," one of the men says, lifting a saw which he moves towards the man's leg.

When I come closer, I see the leg is badly mangled. Nathaniel moves to the table and places two fingers on the man's forehead. I feel the magic rise and there's a momentary flash of white light and the man calms.

"Thank you," one of the doctors says before setting to his grim work.

"Nate," I call out.

He looks over, his eyes hollow and haunted, but I see a hint of warmth in them. He leans down and whispers something to the man on the table before walking over.

"What are you doing?" I ask.

"Helping, the best I can anyway," he shrugs.

Grimacing, I nod. It's overwhelming how many people are here. The worst part is the one thing I know that they don't. They won't fit on the train.

"We have to save them," I say.

His head jerks towards me sharply. He grabs my arm, gripping it tight, and pulls me out of the area. He pulls me along until we're in a recessed alcove, away from prying eyes. It's a tight space, and our bodies are pressing against each other, but there's nothing intimate in the look on his face.

"You know what's going to happen," he says.

"We can't…" I start, but I stop myself.

Of course, we can. There's no stopping the flood of memories of people I've left behind already. Black depression lays into me and threatens to swallow me whole. Tears well in my eyes, and one drops down my cheek. Before I can wipe it, Nathaniel wipes it away, then he pulls me into an embrace.

One hand in my hair, the other on the small of my back, he holds me while the tears fall. I can't hold them back. It's too much to confront. There has to be something, anything I can do for them.

"Shhh," he soothes. "Shhh."

"Nate," I sob.

"I know," he says, pulling back and lifting my head with two fingers under my chin. "I know."

That haunted look behind his eyes tells all that needs to be said.

"How do you… deal with it?" I ask.

"Always move forward," he says. "It's the greatest good for the greatest number. Your heart is big, Aviella. Maybe too big, but that makes you special."

"I'm tired of being special," I say. "Why? Why me? I'm not special, why is it we're always saving me and losing so many? Why is the Shadow always one step ahead of us? Why can't we catch a damn break!"

"The journey is long and hard," he says. "One day at a time, that is how you do it. One day, one choice at a time."

His smile is soft as he wipes the tears from my cheek. Leaning down he kisses my forehead, holding me close against him. Our magics flow and intertwine.

He wants me. His passion and fire burns hot against my skin, but now isn't the time. Knowing it is comfort enough and pushes aside my fears that he was no longer mine. He's been avoiding me, but it must be for reasons of his own other than that.

It's difficult navigating the waters I find myself in. Each of my men must be cared for in their own way. They each have needs that I must meet. I wrap my arms around the angel and pull him close, and then I lay my head on his chest.

It's the first time, I think, I've thought of my relationship with the boys in that way. I've been so worried about them being jealous or upset or angry, that I hadn't really looked at what I give to them. Besides amazing sex of course.

Nate runs his fingers through my hair, and we hold each other for a while, until at last it feels like time to move. After releasing him, I lean back against the cold metal of the wall behind me.

"What did you see out there?" I ask.

He frowns, his brow furrowing deeply, and that haunted look comes back to his eyes.

"It's bad," he says.

"Yeah," I exhale. "I tried to find you, once. To reach out to you in the dream realms. I thought I came close, but couldn't reach you."

"Don't do that," he admonishes me. "It's more dangerous than you can possibly know."

"Tell me about it," I say, shaking my head.

He touches my face and trails his fingers along my jaw. I'm leaning back against the wall, and he's doing the same, pressing our waists against each other. His manhood presses hard into my belly, but neither of us shift away.

"We should help more," he says, not moving.

"We should," I agree, but my body is burning for an entirely different kind of help.

Subtly I move, only a little side-to-side motion. Nate's jaw tenses and his eyes widen, but still he doesn't move away. I bite my lower lip, struggling to stay in control of the base urges raging through my body.

He places his hands on my sides and slowly they drift up, closer to my breasts. I inhale sharply, wanting, no needing him to take them in his hands. I arch my back, pushing them forward in invitation. Please Nate, give me this, I need you.

"Nathaniel!" Silas's voice echoes outside our hidden alcove.

It cuts through and kills the moment. We both straighten quickly. I look around, feeling suddenly guilty, of what, I don't even know. Nate steps out of the alcove and I follow him, fixing my shirt as I do.

Silas is turning in a circle fifty feet away and calls for Nate again.

"Here!" Nate calls, raising a hand and waving at Silas.

Silas smiles when he sees Nate, and then something passes across his face when he sees I'm with him. He rushes through the carefully arranged cots and those milling about tending them.

"What are you doing down here?" he asks me, his voice harsh.

"Helping, what are you doing?" I challenge back.

His face darkens further. "This is dangerous and stupid. Where is Efram? He's supposed to be watching you."

Silas looks around as if expecting Efram to materialize out of thin air.

"I'm not a child," I say angrily. "I don't need a 'watcher' or anyone else to look after me. Besides I'm with Nate."

The look on Silas's face says it all. My blood runs hot as I step closer to him ready to give him more than a piece of my mind.

"What's happening?" Efram says from behind me.

I jerk around, anger lost in the surprise of him being there at this exact moment. Efram looks innocent, but the timing is crazy.

"Did you arrange this?" I ask, looking at Silas and Nate. They both shake their heads. "Gah! What now?"

"The evacuation is in the morning," Efram says.

My stomach drops to the floor and cold sweat forms. Two hours. I look past my gathered boys at the sick and wounded surrounding us and I swallow hard and shudder. They're all going to be left behind. There's no room for any of them.

"Shit," I say.

Nate places a comforting hand on my shoulder. Warmth flows from him into me. He's using his magic to try and reas-

193

sure me, assuage the feelings of guilt he must know I'm feeling. The haunted look in his eyes says he's done this too many times.

Efram and Silas move closer too, the three of them enclosing me, encompassing me with their bodies as well as their magic. I close my eyes and draw off their support. Each of them flows power to me in their own ways, both magical and otherwise.

"There has to be a way," I mutter, not opening my eyes as I try to imagine any scenario that ends with us saving all the people of this Bunker.

None of them speak. There isn't one and we all know it. It's up to me to come to terms with it, somehow.

Efram places a hand on my lower back, Nate's hand on my shoulder, then Silas touches my side. The three of them touching me, soft, innocent yet intimate. Focusing on those points of contact gives me strength. They anchor me and together we'll get through, somehow.

"You should eat," Efram says breaking the moment.

My stomach grumbles loudly in agreement. Together we leave the sick bay area and head up the levels back towards my rooms, where there will be food waiting. There's a heavy layer of dread across the entirety of the Bunker. We move through it but it's a thick miasma that we have to push past.

The people know. No one's told them, and they may not acknowledge it consciously, but no matter the petty games they've played, they know what's going to happen. The rumors of the evacuation have spread throughout. They know, but if they admit to it, then the panic will set in, and they can't face that either.

We get to my rooms and the mood is somber. Efram helps me in the kitchen, and we make some quick food for all of us. We sit and eat, quiet still.

"I'm leaving," Silas says. "Tynan has asked me to scout ahead in the Mega-Church Bunker."

"What?" I ask, my voice cracking.

"I'm the best for the job, and if we're going there next, we need to get the lay of the land," he says.

"You can't," I say, shaking my head. "Alone? No way."

"I can, and I must," Silas says.

"He's right, Aviella," Nate says.

"No," I respond, but I'm being petulant and childish. "Damn it."

"It's smart. He really is best for this job," Efram says. "We need the lay of the land."

It takes me a minute to get the swirling red rage under control completely.

"We're always a move behind," I say, slamming a fist into my open hand. "We have to get ahead of the Shadow forces. We have to!"

No one argues. Nate wraps his arms around me from behind, and Silas and Efram enclose me the rest of the way. No one speaks because words aren't necessary. Their presence is comforting, giving me an emotional support that is accented by the flow of our magics intertwining with each other.

I raise my head towards Silas, and on an urge, I kiss him. A soft, gentle, but passionate kiss that he returns. The other two men's hands begin to roam as desire flares between the four of us, and I give myself over to the welcome sensations.

Hands slide under my shirt, touching my skin, which fevers at the contact. Other hands are on my ass, still more stroke my breasts through the cloth. Silas's tongue drives into my mouth, my own greeting it.

When I break my kiss with him, I turn my head to find Efram's waiting mouth and continue kissing. My body thrums with building desire. One hand on Efram's chest, I

195

trail my other down Silas's chest towards his waist, finding the waiting bulge that I rub through his pants.

Nate presses against my back, his rock-hard cock rubbing against me. He lowers himself so that he's pressing it against my ass. Moaning, I push into him, ready for them to take me.

The door to my room opens, but I'm only dimly aware of it.

"Looks like I arrived just in time!" Rafe exclaims.

I jerk away from the men and run leaping into his arms. Rafe catches me easily, laughing as he spins me around.

"Rafe!" I exclaim.

"Well, hello to you too," he says.

Riding the wave of passion and desire, I kiss the demon. He returns the kiss, grabbing my ass, his dick pressing against me. Tangling my hands in his hair, I continue the kiss as long as I can before I have to break for breath.

"I've missed you," I gasp.

"Wouldn't have guessed it," he says.

When I've unwrapped my legs from his waist and I'm standing on my own again, I keep an arm around him as I turn to face the others. My cheeks flush as it hits me what I did and how many men are here. I'm still getting used to this situation.

"Welcome back," Efram says, walking over with an extended hand that Rafe takes, then jerks him forward into a manly embrace.

Rafe pats Efram's back, then lets him go. Silas and Rafe embrace next, then Rafe and Nate are staring at each other. Opposite sides of the same coin, the relationship between the demon and the angel has always been… interesting.

"Don't hug me," Nate says, his voice deadpan.

"Yeah," Rafe nods. "Might ruffle your feathers, huh?"

"I'm glad you're back," Nate responds, a concession for the angel to admit as much.

"I knew you'd miss me." Rafe grins broadly, and then he grabs Nate and pulls him into an embrace.

Nate stiffens, resisting the demon's hug, so Rafe, being Rafe, pushes it. He leans his head back, still holding the stiff-as-a-board Nate, and plants a kiss right on his lips. My eyes widen and my mouth drops open in surprise. Deep in my core, the fire burns hotter. It's the hottest, strangest thing I've ever seen.

Nate jerks free, ending the moment. "Damn it, Rafe."

Efram and Silas laugh and Rafe joins them.

"Oh, Nate," he says, shaking his head. "So, what have I missed?"

He looks at each of us in turn.

"You'd better sit down," I say, motioning to the sitting area.

We all take seats, and I lead the way, briefing Rafe on what he's missed. I gloss over that I've slept with the dragons and Silas. There's no need to rub that in any of their faces. None of those who know bother to bring it up, so let's let that dog lie for now.

"A lot indeed," Rafe says when I finish. "So the Shadow forces have penetrated the Bunker?"

"Yeah," I say.

"That's bad," he muses, shifting in the chair and throwing a leg over one arm while leaning further back into it.

Rafe has a way of unconsciously posing himself to the best effect. The way he's lying pulls his shirt up, revealing the hard ab muscles the clothing hides, and he hooks his hands behind his head, putting the bulging biceps to best effect. My mouth dries, and I swallow hard, trying to force moisture back.

"What about you?" I ask, forcing myself to focus while doing my best to suppress the tingling energy flowing through my body. "What did you find?"

A darkness passes over his face, and his eyes take on a red glow. It's only a moment but I don't miss it, and I don't think anyone else here does.

"It's bad," he says.

"Well, yeah, another trumpet," I say.

"Worse," he says. "The Shadow forces are working openly, setting the path for the world."

His words brings silence. All of us look at each other, but no one has anything to say or add. I realize they're all looking at me, and it hits me. All of this depends on me. My shoulders slump under the weight of it.

Me.

It's all on me.

"Aviella, sweet baby, you can do this," my Dad's voice whispers in my head.

Warmth forms in my core, and I straighten up in my chair. I meet each of their gazes, and first I smile, then nod.

"Right," I say. "We've got work to do."

I speak with a confidence I don't really feel, but hey, fake it till you make it, right? There's no other choice.

"We're going to the Mega-Church next," Silas says.

"Seriously?" Rafe growls.

"Yes," Silas says. "We have information they are holding a group of Innocents they've been able to hide from the mages."

"And my Dad," I interject, firmly.

"And possibly Aviella's' father," Silas acknowledges.

Rafe frowns, then nods. "I can't enter there."

"Shit," I say. No one else speaks. "All right, well that is, what it is. What do we do next? The trains leave in the morning. Silas, when are you leaving?"

"I'll leave in an hour or so," he says. "I'll use a gate and be there long before you arrive."

"What about the dragons? Any word on their plans yet?" I ask.

"They have a mission of their own," Silas says. "They're not going to the next Bunker immediately. They may already be gone."

"What?" I ask, shocked. "Why didn't they tell me?"

"Probably because you'd try to stop them, and who among us could stand against you?" Rafe asks.

I look at him in utter surprise. The other guys look at the floor or the walls, anywhere but at me.

"What do you mean?" I ask.

Rafe swings his legs off the arm of the chair and leans towards me.

"You," he says, his voice soft and almost serious, "are the center, Aviella. I went through hell, literally, for you. Nate, Efram, Silas, yes, even the Horsemen of the Apocalypse, the dragons, do it all for you.

You're special and you know it. We know it. We're bound to you in ways I don't think any of us fully understand. Our fates intertwine and twist together, all around your beautiful, perfect pinky finger."

He grabs my hand quick as lightning and raises it to his lips. Slowly, seductively, he places my index finger in his mouth, sucking on it while his eyes bore into mine. The fire burning in him flows through the room, affecting all of us.

"Rafe," I force his name past the lump in my throat.

My desire is burning so hot it dries my mouth. I can't swallow, can't think, can't take my eyes off his. His tongue moves around my finger as he slowly pulls backwards. It pops as it exits his mouth. His smile is intoxicating, and I lose myself in him.

Magic swirls, flowing around until it encompasses all the men. They're drawn in, pulled to me. Efram is the only one who holds back, but one glance, and I see his desire.

Someone pulls my shirt over my head, and then I lean in, kissing Rafe.

Silas kneels on one side, and Nate has moved to the opposite. Their hands roam across my bare skin, each of them taking a breast and kneading it softly. As one, they take my nipples in their mouths, and I groan into Rafe's mouth.

Their attention to my breasts turns the fire in my core to a raging inferno. I need them.

Someone undoes my pants, and as they do I grab Rafe's and jerk them open. His cock bulges out, and I reach into his underwear to grab it.

A hand finds its way under my own, sliding across my mound and piercing my wet and ready tunnel. I push forward with my hips to drive that finger deeper while gripping Rafe's large cock tighter and stroking.

They continue their attention on my tits, the hand in my pussy, and I throw my head back exclaiming my pleasure. Efram watches from his chair, and now has his stiff member in his hand, slowly moving up and down.

Rafe grabs my hair and jerks my head to him, kissing me again.

Someone slides my pants down over my ass and then slaps it. The loud smack and instant of pain accents and plays off the multiple points of pleasure, heightening them.

I reach out for Efram, and he takes my hand, squeezing.

Someone grabs my neck and pushes me towards Rafe, and the bending at my waist thrusts my ass out. A cock positions at my opening, and I'm ready for it, need it.

The room rocks so hard, all of us are thrown around. A trumpeting sound blares so loud, my ears are left ringing as I pick myself up off the floor.

CHAPTER TWENTY-TWO

AVIELLA

"What was that?" I'm probably screaming, but I can't tell because the ringing in my ears is so loud.

As I climb to my feet, the room is rocked again, and I'm thrown onto my face, smashing my nose and tasting blood in my mouth.

I'm pulled to my feet and held steady. Rafe and Nate have me from either side. I wipe blood off my mouth and look around, my anger rising.

I pull my pants up and grab my shirt while the boys throw on their clothes too. In moments, we're racing out the door. Smoke billows down the hall outside my rooms. It's so thick I can't see through it, but that doesn't stop me. I run headlong towards it.

"Aviella, wait!" Efram yells, but the screams of the hurt and dying pull me forward.

Those cries of pain and terror call me. They need me, I have to help. Ignoring Efram, I continue forward.

When I pass through the checkpoint, with smoke swirling

around us blocking our vision, a strange cool breeze passes over me. I've never felt a breeze here.

"Guys? You feel that?" I ask, then the breeze comes again, pushing the smoke aside, and I realize the source. The roof is gone, torn away, exposing the open night sky above.

The loud trumpeting roar sounds again, deafening me. Hands land on my shoulders, and I instinctively jump away before realizing it's Rafe and Silas. Efram and Nate are right behind them, yelling. I see their mouths moving, but I can't hear the words over the ringing in my ears.

Shaking my head negative, I point at my ears. Efram leaps, flying at me. Before I can react, he hits me in the chest, knocking me to the ground. Flames blast through the space I was standing in, engulfing Rafe and Silas.

"RAFE! SILAS!" I scream loud enough to hear myself over the ringing.

The flames die down and Rafe is standing with an outraged look on his face. His clothes are burnt and smoking, black holes through them. His mouth moves angrily as he raises his hands. Black-red magic forms around his fists and he thrusts them forward sending the demonic energy racing down the hall.

Efram helps me to my feet. My head is spinning and I'm weaving, unable to stand straight. Efram takes me by my shoulders, and then Nate is there. He grabs my head between his hands and a white glow fills my vision.

"Hold that thing back!" Silas yells as my hearing suddenly returns.

When I turn in the direction he's looking, the first thing I see is Rafe running. Smoke and burning debris fill the hallway. Something moves overhead, pulling my attention up. A... thing looks into the opening where the roof should be.

It's a diamond-shaped head, almost snake-like if a snake's head was as big as me. It has cold, onyx eyes and a darting, forked tongue. The head is on a long, sinewy neck that sways back and forth. The thing opens its mouth, revealing what looks like thousands of needle-sharp teeth in concentric rows. It roars, the sound echoing off the walls, and bouncing around us, pounding against my chest, making it hard to breath.

Whatever Nate did to heal my ears holds true because I'm not deafened again, thankfully. Rafe skids to a stop under the thing's head. It darts at him, snapping its jaws, obviously trying to take a bite out of the demon.

Rafe dodges to one side, slamming his black-red-covered fist into its head. It screams, this time in pain. Viscous green goo flies from it, then it pulls its head out of the hole.

"We have to get people on the trains," I yell.

"There's no time," Silas says.

"We'll make time!" I yell, turning and bursting into a run.

They can keep up, or they can fall behind. I'm not leaving all these people behind. I have to save them, or as many as I can. It's not a nicety or an option, damn it. I'm sick of leaving people behind.

As we enter the main levels, the panic-stricken crowds grow into a knotted mass of humanity. Screams of fear tear up the air as they stampede from one area to the next, running without direction or purpose.

My men and I come to a stop as I survey the scene. If we don't get them under some kind of control, we'll lose all of them. Magic pulses through my limbs and veins. I reach out to pull in more, drawing on each of the guys with me, until a burning sensation fills me.

"Listen!" I yell, my voice booms over their noise reverberating off the walls.

Along with it, I push out my will that they all shut up and calm down. Silence falls so fast, it's like someone hit the mute button. The crowds turn towards me, but I can't be seen. I'm too short. I don't have to say anything, Efram and Silas lift me onto their shoulders. Now I'm not only able to be seen, but I can see around the entire open area.

"The trains are one level down. Make your way there. Do not push, do not run, help each other!"

They look at me like I'm insane. Their wide eyes and slack-jawed expressions show that they barely comprehend my words. Damn it.

"Allow me," Rafe says, stepping forward.

He appears to grow as he walks to them, red-black energy swirling around him as wings sprout from his back. He appears to be around eight feet tall and the crowd reacts to the sight of a demon coming at them. They turn and stampede away. At least they're going in the right direction, albeit not in the organized, kind manner I'd hoped. I'll take it.

Rafe turns around, looking his normal self, with his full-of-himself grin plastered across his face. I roll my eyes at him, then motion after the crowd, and we run along behind them.

It isn't long before fresh screams reach our ears, and then the crowd is stampeding back up the hall towards us. Nate throws me against the wall, and the four men form a protective barrier keeping me pressed tight as the crowd pushes their way past.

"Damn it, we have to get them to the trains!" I yell.

"Aviella," Silas says, "it doesn't matter. There won't be room for them."

Bile rises in my throat as I open my mouth to protest, but his hard eyes won't let me lie to him or myself any longer. Swallowing down the sick, tears run from my eyes, but I nod, forcing myself to accept the reality.

"Right," I say, a shudder racing down my spine.

The crowd is past us, so Efram takes one arm and Silas

the other. Nate and Rafe stalk the hallway in front of us. My knights of light and darkness, clearing the path.

Now that I have steeled my resolve, we set off at a run. The halls are mostly empty now, the majority of the crowds having run the other way, and in moments we find out why. Racing around a corner we come face to face with a conglomerated mass of a nightmare given form.

Roiling black flesh, tiny hands and mouths full of teeth protrude from everywhere. It fills the hall, rolling towards us like a black ball of doom. My stomach revolts at the wrongness of it. It makes a mewling sound like a hundred sick cats that makes my skin crawl.

"What in the name of—" I'm cut off before I can finish the thought.

Black ichor spews out of it, sizzling as it flies through the air. Where bits of it land, there's a sizzling sound as it burns through anything it touches. Nate crosses his arms in front of himself, and a shimmering white shield forms, blocking the hall. The black ichor lands on it and slides down, burning into the floor and creating a crevasse.

Rafe summons a sword, which has black flames licking up and down its length, then Nate summons his own which is sheathed in gold-white flame. The angel and the demon charge the thing and attack with lightning-quick motions.

I close my eyes and focus on the buzz deep in my core— my magic comes easily now as I shape it to do my will. In my mind's eye, I imagine a shield encasing the thing then growing smaller. When I open my eyes, the thing is smaller and growing smaller as I watch. Nate and Rafe continue their attacks until the thing pops loudly and would explode, but my magical shield contains it, keeping Rafe and Nate safe from the acidic spray.

The two of them look back, grateful, and then we're running. There are random trumpet creatures in the halls, but we're able to avoid any confrontation. We're leaving, and fighting them now is an exercise in futility.

When we get to the level the trains are on, there are guards, holding a line. Crowds of people press up against them, shouting and waving money and things, as if they can buy their way past them. One of the guards sees us and makes a motion. More guards join them and they use their bodies to create a tunnel through the crowd. We walk the tunnel and run for the trains.

Glancing over my shoulder I'm sick with the decision I'm having to make. I stop. I can't do this. I can't leave them behind to fight on their own. The boys group around me and they know my unspoken thoughts. Nathaniel places a comforting hand on my shoulder.

"Aviella," he says, his voice soft and filled with emotions. "We could do this. We might win, but it's a big maybe. If we do, we risk everything."

"I've been out there," Rafe says. "This is nothing compared to what's coming. Aviella, trust me, we have to have our eye on the bigger picture. We have to stop the Shadow forces, and right now they're winning."

"They're winning another bunker," I say, tears falling freely. "I can stop them. Here, now, I can stop them."

"No, you can't," Silas says. "You're not strong enough... yet."

"We're with you, Aviella," Efram says, and the unspoken agreement of the others comes with his words. "It's your choice—but they're right. This is, in the bigger scheme, unwinnable. Even if we do stop this invasion, they'll send more."

"It's your choice, kiddo," Rafe says. "You say fight, we'll do it, no matter if it's the right thing or not."

"Damn it," I say, my voice hoarse.

I turn to the trains. The weight of the world is on my

shoulders, and I feel every single ounce of it. Climbing onto that train is the hardest thing I've ever done in my life. There's been nothing to compare. I stare out the window to memorize the faces I see. They deserve to be remembered. I'm sacrificing them for a future for our entire race.

I'm an asshole.

≈

Continue *the Power of Twelve* series in book four, **Apocalypse the Betrayal**

ABOUT THE AUTHOR

USA Today Bestselling Author of fantasy and scifi romance, Miranda Martin's books feature larger than life heroes with out-of-this-world anatomy and smart heroines destined to save the world. As a little girl she would sneak off with her nose in a book, dreaming of magical realms. Today she brings those fantasies to life and adores every fan who chooses to live in them for a while.

She was born and raised in southern Virginia, but as a veteran she's traveled to places like Korea, Hawaii and good 'ole Texas. Now she's settled in Kansas, the heart of America, with her husband and daughters. Her favorite animals are dragons, unicorns and cats. If she's not writing, you can still find her tucked away somewhere with a warm blanket and her nose in a book.

Get in touch!
mirandamartinromance.com
miranda@mirandamartinromance.com

facebook.com/mirandamartin
twitter.com/imMirandaMartin
instagram.com/imMirandaMartin

www.ingramcontent.com/pod-product-compliance
Lightning Source LLC
Chambersburg PA
CBHW051649260626
47170CB00004B/1405